"No way in hell."

Andi stared in horror at the full-length mirror before her. It had seemed like a good idea when Jesse had mentioned being the new hostess for the national syndication of *Revved Up*. He said the network and the show's new producer wanted to bring a woman onto the show, and he wanted someone who knew their way around cars. Andi fit the bill for both, and she would love to have a hand in planning the custom jobs. This was her chance to step up her game.

That was before she'd seen the wardrobe for her new role in the garage. She'd worked at Kasen's Kustom for a couple of years, and she loved what she did. Really loved it. It was fun and challenging to turn classic cars back into the cherry rides they had once been, while adding a few extra modernizations. She'd loved it even more when they'd turned the garage's work into a reality show. But she was a background player in all of it, and she wanted to show them what she could really do.

Apparently, that meant she had to learn how to walk in high heels.

Revved Up

COMPLETE SERIES

C. JORDAN

Contents

Author's Note

My husband and I have a fascination for car restoration TV shows, especially those that deal with vintage and classic cars, so this series is my way of putting all those hours of binge-watching to good use. I hope you enjoy getting to know the Kasen cousins and the women who steal their hearts.

All Revved Up

REVVED UP, BOOK 1

C. JORDAN

CJ BOOKS

Chapter 1

Reno, Nevada

"No way in hell, Jesse." Dean Kasen tossed a pencil down on his desk and glared at his cousin. "I went along with it when you wanted to turn the garage into a reality TV show, but—"

"And business has never been better, has it?" Arching a blond eyebrow, Jesse offered up an incredulous stare, as if he had no idea why Dean might be upset.

Dean growled, refusing to give an inch. This was his family's legacy at stake, and he wasn't about to let anyone screw that up, not even a member of his family. They owned equal shares of Kasen's Kustom Automotive, so this wasn't the first time they'd had to duke it out over disagreements on how the garage should be run. Dean drummed his fingers on the desk. "Business is good, yeah. But that doesn't mean—"

"They want to give *Revved Up* national syndication, Dean!" Jesse pinched the bridge of his nose, looking as annoyed as Dean felt. "This is a *good* thing, and you were into it until this morning."

"That's because until this morning, I didn't know the network wanted to boost our ratings by letting some dimwit in a short skirt loose in my garage. I am not letting them turn this place into a joke. I've worked—*we've* worked—too damn hard to keep Kasen's a reputable name to blow it now."

Jesse threw his hands up in the air, and his chair squeaked as he flopped back. "Fine. You're right."

"I know I'm right." Dean narrowed his eyes. His cousin had never given up on an argument that quickly in his entire life. There had to be a catch.

A charming grin flashed across the other man's face, and Dean knew he was in trouble. Damn it. He sighed and scrubbed a hand over the back of his neck. What now?

Jesse's grin grew to a broad smile. "I knew you'd get bent out of shape about this, so I already came up with a compromise I know you'll agree to."

Grunting, Dean picked up the pencil and tapped it on his desktop. "So? Let's hear it if you're that sure."

"I can do better than that. I'll show you." Jesse heaved himself out of the chair he was sprawled in and strode to the door, poking his head out to talk to someone Dean couldn't see. "Hey, come on in and…uh, *whoa!*"

"**N**o way in hell."

Andi stared in horror at the full-length mirror before

her. It had seemed like a good idea when Jesse had mentioned being the new hostess for the national syndication of *Revved Up*. He said the network and the show's new producer wanted to bring a woman onto the show, and he wanted someone who knew their way around cars. Andi fit the bill for both, and she would love to have a hand in planning the custom jobs. This was her chance to step up her game.

That was before she'd seen the wardrobe for her new role in the garage. She'd worked at Kasen's Kustom for a couple of years, and she loved what she did. Really loved it. It was fun and challenging to turn classic cars back into the cherry rides they had once been, while adding a few extra modernizations. She'd loved it even more when they'd turned the garage's work into a reality show. But she was a background player in all of it, and she wanted to show them what she could really do. Apparently, that meant she had to learn how to walk in high heels. Jesse had handed her off to the new producer, Lola Adams, who'd stuffed her into too-tight clothes, tugged her hair out of its usual ponytail, pulled out the biggest makeup kit Andi had ever seen, and teased and dabbed and swabbed and slathered and powdered. Now she just stared at the stranger who used to be Andi Manning. For thirty whole seconds.

"No way in hell." She stumbled back, holding out her hands as if to ward off her own reflection.

Lola tilted her head, her pale hair spilling over her shoulder. Her Southern accent made her voice roll out as thick and sweet as molasses. "I think it works. You look sexy and that's what we're going for. I think it'll bring in even more viewers now that we're taking the show to the next level."

Mouth gaping open, Andi couldn't even find the words to respond to that. The coveralls she was wearing were cut into tight shorts that were opened to the waist. The tank top underneath stretched across her breasts and was just short enough to expose an inch of her midriff. Her brown hair fell in smooth ripples to the middle of her back. All the makeup Lola had piled on Andi's face somehow made her hazel eyes stand out and appear more gold than their usual brownish-green.

The woman in the mirror was no one she knew.

Spinning on her heel meant she damn near toppled over in the pointy stilettos that cramped her toes, but she marched out of the dressing area and into the garage. A few of the guys let out low whistles, and she gave them a glare that silenced them and sent them scurrying to find work to do.

Jesse poked his blond head out of the office, his green eyes going wide for a moment before he caught her gaze. Whatever he said faltered as he must have sensed the pissed off waves coming off her. He stumbled away from the door while she shoved her way in and slammed it behind her.

"What the hell is this, Jesse? Is this some kind of joke to you? Because I sure don't appreciate you jerking me around." Yeah, he was her boss. At the moment, she didn't care. He'd said he wanted to add her to the show for her *professional expertise* and then had her walking around half-naked. She somehow doubted her professionalism was what people would notice in this getup.

There was dead silence while both men in the room stared at her, their jaws sagging a bit. She jammed her hands down on her hips. *"What?"*

Jesse recovered first, coughing into his fist. "Nothing. You just look different."

"I look like I work at the Mustang Ranch," she shot back, naming a famous local brothel. There was nothing wrong with sex work, but it wasn't her line of work. Auto shops tended to require a bit more in the way of clothing, what with all the grease and chemicals lying around.

Show hosting had better come with hazard pay.

Dean snorted, a little smile kicking up the corner of his mouth. He sat at his desk, watching the scene unfold between his cousin and her, but then his gaze slid down her body and back up again. Slowly. An involuntary shiver went through her at the heat in his gaze. How many times had she wondered what it would be like for Dean Kasen to look at her in just that way? Her mouth went dry, her stomach flipped, and she shivered again.

"Um..." Jesse said, brushing a hand through his golden hair.

The man looked like a fallen angel, blond and more gorgeous than anyone had a right to be. But his cousin was the devil to his angel. The only thing the two men had in common was their bright green eyes. Andi couldn't take her eyes off of Dean as he sprawled in his office chair, his hands folded behind his head. His muscular shoulders were impossibly wide, tapering to lean hips. His black hair was just a bit shaggy, his skin tanned. He had sex appeal coming out of his pores, and Andi's body warmed the way it always did when she was around him.

"I think you look sexy." His lids dropped to half-mast. "I think that's what they were going for, right?"

There was something *she'd* definitely go for, and it included him using that low rumble on her. All night long. She quashed the thought as she always did. Dean was her boss, and until this very second, he'd never given her a second glance. Nope, that was her little fantasy, wasn't it? She tugged at the bottom of her nonexistent top. "It's really not my style at all."

"I know it's not, but the network is looking for an attractive woman to join the crew the viewers see. Our new producer thinks you'll be great at it, and so do we." Jesse jumped back into the conversation, as if he sensed her weakening. "Just give it a chance and see if you can get used to it. If not, we'll find another solution."

Another solution that probably meant she wouldn't get a freer hand in helping design the overhauls. She didn't care for that at all. Now that the opportunity had been put in front of her, she wanted it. She wanted it bad. Enough to dress like this? Doubt wavered within her. Could she really do this? On national television? Her friends and family would see her dressed this way. Her very conservative grandmother would *definitely* make comments.

"We do think you'll be good at this," Dean said. "*I* think you'll be good at this. You're one of my best mechanics, and I'd love to see you more involved in the projects we do for the show, instead of the off-screen work." Dean's voice was smooth, warm honey sliding over her skin. His gaze stayed on her face as he spoke, letting her know he meant it, but that didn't hide the heat that lingered in his gaze. "Give it two weeks. If you still hate it, well then..." His voice trailed off, leaving the thought unfinished. But the way he looked at her made her insides melt. He looked as if he liked what he saw, as if he wanted to eat her up, maybe lick her from head to toe.

Passion exploded through her at that thought, and her sex went hot and wet in moments. Jesus, what she wouldn't give to have him keep looking at her this way. But she *could* have that, couldn't she? All she had to do was show up for work every day, let Lola do her thing with the makeup and wardrobe, *and* Andi would get the career bump she desperately wanted. Put in that light, it made it pretty simple, didn't it? Still, a quiver passed through her, and she felt as if she were stepping off a cliff with no way of knowing how far she'd fall or how bad the landing would be. She pulled in a deep breath, logic and lust wrestling for dominance inside her.

She had no idea which one won out when she said, "Okay, I'll give it the two weeks."

Chapter 2

"This is a 1949 Volkswagen Beetle, which most of us just call a Bug," Andi said. "Unfortunately, this car has seen better days. It's spent a little too much time in the snow where they salt the roads, which has corroded and rusted out the undercarriage of the vehicle." She opened up the driver's side door and pointed to a spot on the floor where you could see right through the metal. She gestured to the rest of the interior and let the cameraman get his shot while she spoke. "The seats and pretty much the entire interior of the car have been used and abused and it shows. We're going to have to gut most of this little Bug and start from scratch. But let me show you something we won't be touching."

Dean watched her in silence, mesmerized by how easily she poured on the charm. He'd seen her turn this on for recalcitrant customers, but never this full-blown show. Jesse was right, she really was perfect for this. He bit back a groan when she leaned forward slightly and her shorts stretched tight across her round little backside.

The camera followed her to the rear of the vehicle where she gestured to the back window. "See how it's actually split into two smaller windows? The Germans thought this looked like the two holes in a pretzel, so they nicknamed this model the 'Pretzel Beetle.' This is a feature that only appears in Bugs from 1946 to 1953. It hampered vision out of the rearview mirror, so it was replaced with the single window we're all used to seeing. During the overhaul, we're going to preserve this unique feature because it shows the true age of this classic."

Lola called out from the sidelines. "Nicely done, Andi. Jesse said you're going to be working with Dean to pull out the old engine—are you ready to show us that?"

"Yep, we're ready."

He damn near groaned at the sight of Andi coming toward him. She was a walking wet dream in those cutoff coveralls, unzipped to bare the creamy skin at her midriff. It went from warm in the garage to scorching hot in under ten seconds as she slid in beside him. She bent to help him finish detaching the motor so they could use the engine crane to lift it out. The rest of the crew started stripping down the car and they answered Lola's questions as they worked, doing their best to ignore the camera and get the job done.

It was many hours later before they called a halt to shooting. The garage staff and film crew packed it up for the night and made beelines for the exit. Only a few stragglers remained when Dean leaned back against the side of the car and dragged his shirt up to wipe the sweat off his face. He couldn't remember it ever being this damn hot in the garage. Having Andi pressed against him for most of the day hadn't helped in the least, but the close quarters of the small VW Bug made it impossible to put some space between them. Jesse had thought the challenge of the little classic would be fun, the producer thought having the show's first female car owner would be a great way to introduce Andi as an added female to the regular crew, and the owner wanted her car tricked out and had paid a lot of money for the chance to have the Kasens of *Revved Up* work on her ride. On television.

None of that had prepared Dean for the fact that he'd spend a lot of uncomfortable hours with a raging hard-on and the desire to drag Andi away from the cameras and get his hands all over her. Jesus, what was wrong with him? Sure, he'd wanted her since the day his father hired her. But he'd known he'd be the boss by the end of that same year when his dad retired, so putting the moves on a woman who worked for the auto shop was a bad idea. And Dean wasn't one to go for bad ideas. He left the crazy schemes to his cousin.

Andi settled beside him, and her hip and arm brushed against his. She crossed her legs at the ankles, the barely-there coveralls riding up on her thighs. "So, how do you think it went? Did I do okay?"

"I think it's going fine." His voice was more clipped than he meant it to be, but every time she moved, she slid against him and his erection throbbed like a toothache that wouldn't quit. He'd never let himself be this close to her for this long. Somehow, he'd known exactly how tempting, how dangerous she'd be to his self-restraint. The sweet, feminine smell of her, the throaty sound of her laugh, the way her smile lit up her entire face. Add that to the almost-outfit she was in and he was doomed. His hands shook with the need to touch that bare skin and see if it was just as soft as he'd always imagined. Clenching his fingers, he dragged his gaze away from her legs.

She put her hand on his arm. "Are you upset about something? You've seemed...off...most of the day."

Heat streaked through him, radiating out from where she touched him. He couldn't do this. There was no way his sanity would survive.

He couldn't have her this near and not break. As good as she might be for the show's ratings, they were going to have to find a woman who didn't drive him mad with lust. They both flinched when a door screeched open and one of the garage crew waved as he headed out. Dean jerked to his feet. "Andi, can I see you in my office?"

"Uh...sure." Uncertainty flashed over her features, but she straightened and followed him.

The tantalizing scent of her filled his nostrils as she passed by to enter the office. He shut the door behind them. If there were any of the guys still here, he didn't want them to overhear this.

"What's wrong, Dean?" She planted her hands on her hips and met his gaze squarely.

That was his Andi—straightforward, no beating around the bush. Only she wasn't *his* Andi and she never would be. The thought only served to make him angry. As turned on as he was, anything that kept him from getting what he wanted pissed him off. He'd been resisting her for far too long, damn it. He hated that he had to.

Her hazel eyes narrowed with temper, her chin tilted stubbornly, and she crossed her arms over her chest. "Well? You had something to say to me, right?"

The challenge was too much for him, firing his blood. The way her cleavage was about to spill out of that top short-circuited his brain. "Nope, I don't have a damn thing to say to you. I have something I want to *do* to you, though."

With that, he reached out, grabbed her arm, and jerked her forward, groaning when her curves fitted against him. Thrusting his fingers into her hair, he gave her a second to protest if she wanted. She didn't. Her hazel eyes locked on his lips, and he couldn't resist kissing her. Soft and sweet. All of her. Just like he'd thought. Her arms curled around his neck and she strained against him.

The encouragement was like offering a banquet to a starving man. He swept his tongue between her lips, and she moaned into his mouth. A tiny part of his mind wondered what in hell he was doing, but then her slender body twisted in his arms, rubbing her breasts over his chest. Fire exploded in his veins, and any sense of reality went out the window. There was no way he could pull back now. He had to have more. Everything.

Tightening his grip on her hair, he pulled her head back, exposing her throat to his lips. He kissed, sucked, and bit his way down her neck, and her nails dug into his shoulders. She whispered, "This is crazy."

Didn't he know it? But he didn't want that reminder, so he sank his teeth into her neck and made her writhe. She lifted one leg and twined it around his hip, arching her body into his.

"Dean! Please, Dean. *More.*"

Her breathless cry, her slim form molded to his, the smell of her desire sent desire shooting through his system. He bit her skin lightly, and a low sob spilled from her. She undulated against him, rubbing herself against him through their clothing. He couldn't wait. He wanted his hands on her naked flesh, his mouth on her breast, and his erection buried deep inside her. Any or all of the above. Right now. Releasing her silky hair, he slipped his fingers down over her brief top, pausing to circle her tight nipple before he moved to the zipper on the front of her coveralls. His knuckles brushed her bare midriff and the rasp of the zipper parting made anticipation grip his gut.

She shrugged out of the top of the coveralls, and he dipped his hand in until he reached her panties. Edging underneath the scrap of cotton, he delved into the soft thatch of hair between her thighs. She whimpered, tightening her leg around his hip, opening herself wider for him. It was an invitation he couldn't resist. Her moisture coated his fingers as he slid up and down her slit, the musky scent of her curling into his nostrils. God, he loved that smell. Lush woman and hot sex. His shaft ached with the need to plunge inside her. Instead, he pushed two fingers into her. "So wet for me, sweetheart."

"Dean," she whispered, a quiver running through her.

Christ, but he loved the sound of his name on her lips, said in that needy little voice. Sweat broke out on his forehead, his heart hammering in his chest. He ran his thumb over her sensitive nub, and her hips bucked against his hand, her hands clenching tight on his shoulders. Sliding his fingers out of her, he plunged them back in. Again and again, building a swift rhythm. She cried out, her body moving in time with his hand, her head thrown back in utter abandon as she gave herself over to him. It was the most erotic thing he'd ever seen. Jesus, he'd never been this hot in his life, and he wasn't even inside her. Leaning in, he caught the tip of her breast in his mouth, sucking her through her thin shirt. When he bit down on the tight little peak, she screamed, her sex fisting around his thrusting fingers.

It was too much. He slid his fingers from her and stepped back just long enough to strip her. Her skin was pale against the thatch of dark curls between her thighs. Her dusky nipples were beaded crests still damp from his mouth, and her slim, bare body looked every bit as gorgeous as he'd ever imagined, framed by the long brown hair that spilled around her shoulders. Yes, that was how he wanted her. Naked and ready for him. Grabbing her arm, he dragged her over to his desk so he could rummage through the top drawer until he came up with the little foil packet he sought.

"You keep condoms in your office?" Andi arched her eyebrows at him, incredulousness flashing over her features. But her hands were busy on his fly, a wicked grin curling her lips. She popped open the button, and slid her hands into his pants, stroking him through his boxers.

"Jesse and I have both gone straight to a date from work once or twice." He barely got the words out over the pleasure rocketing through him. If she kept that up, he wasn't going to last long enough to make this much fun for her. "It's a good idea to be prepared."

"Yeah, you're a real couple of Boy Scouts." Her eyes sparkled with laughter. She slipped her hand down the front of his underwear, and his hips jerked at the first contact of her fingers on his shaft. He had to clench his teeth to keep from coming then and there. She grinned. "Let's get that condom on you."

A laugh spilled out of him. "I like you so much."

It was probably the most honest thing he'd ever said to her, though she'd never know it since they were in the middle of getting busy. He suppressed that thought and, to distract himself, he swooped down and caught her lips with his. She shoved her tongue into his mouth, and the kiss went feral. It was all lips and teeth and tongue, struggling for control of the moment. He cupped one of her breasts, chafed the tip with his thumb, pinched and rolled it between his fingers. She whimpered, pumping his erection hard and driving him to the edge of madness.

"Condom," he growled. "Now."

Those hazel eyes fluttered, glazed with passion. "I thought you'd never ask."

He chuckled, then hissed in a breath when she took the rubber from him, tore the wrapper with her teeth, and had him sheathed in no time. Grabbing her shoulders, he turned her around and bent her over the desk. He rubbed the head of his erection up and down her wet slit, then eased the bulbous crest into her. Their groans echoed in the small room, and he sank deep inside her slick heat. He had to grit his teeth to keep a little control. Damn, this was good. Pulling back, he plunged into her again. And again. His thrusts picked up speed and force. There was no way he could be gentle now. It felt as if electricity shot through him, sizzling his nerve endings. He took her hard and fast, with little finesse, just a driving need to get as deep inside her as possible.

She didn't seem to mind. No, she was right there with him every second, pressing her hips back to meet him halfway. "Oh, God, I'm so close."

"Andi." Her name. It was the only thing he could think to say, his mind unable to wrap itself around the carnal pleasure pounding through him. He just needed her, needed more, needed it now. He leaned forward, twined his fingers with hers and pinned her in place. He turned his head and bit her shoulder.

A scream wrenched from her, and her sex contracted once. Hard. The breath seized in his lungs, a shudder passing through him. He bucked his hips, hilting himself inside her. It was too much, and the tenuous hold he had on his self-control snapped. "Come for me, Andi. Now."

"Yes!" She arched higher, pressing herself closer to him. Her breathing was as ragged as his, and he groaned every time he thrust into her hot, tight core. Her inner muscles clamped around his shaft, and he thought his skull might explode. Her body tensed, and he knew the moment orgasm took her. Her fingers clenched around his, her body undulating as he rode her through her climax, dragging it out for her. "Dean! Oh, my God. *Dean!*"

He broke. Sinking deep inside of her, he stopped fighting orgasm and came harder than he ever had in his life. Heart hammering so loudly it drowned out all other sounds, he kept rocking into her as the high went on and on. Groans wrenched out of him and he shuddered, finally spent.

He watched as Andi turned her head and rested her cheek against the desk, sighing. Her skin was flushed, a satiated smile curving her lips. She was the most beautiful thing he'd ever seen. He opened his mouth to say something, but he couldn't find the words. There was nothing to say. Reality crashed around him, the way he'd known it would. He shouldn't have done this. He knew it. But he refused to let himself regret it. He refused to say something stupid and make this something *she* regretted, so he kept his mouth shut.

Instead, he dropped his forehead to rest between her shoulder blades and drank in the scent of her. So sweet and uniquely Andi, now mingled with the smell of hot sex and him. He liked that far more than he should.

The truth was he'd loved every second of this, but the reasons he'd avoided touching her hadn't changed. Damn it.

"So, how was it?" Taylor leaned forward, her blue eyes gleaming with curiosity.

A blush scorched Andi's cheeks as she stared across the diner table at her best friend. "How, um...how was what?"

How had she known? Was it stamped on her forehead that she'd knocked boots with Dean Kasen the night before? Jesus, she hoped not. The guys at work didn't need to know about this. Whatever "this" was. It had been mind-blowing, and that was about all she'd been able to wrap her mind around in the last twenty-four hours. Dean had been away from the garage today, picking up the new engine they needed for the Bug in Sacramento. She'd have to deal with him tomorrow, so she needed to get her mind wrapped around the facts fast.

Taylor arched an eyebrow. "Oh, really?"

"Really what?" Flushing deeper, Andi brushed a hand down her shirt. What there was of it. She'd come straight from the garage to meet her friend and was still wearing what only the most generous of people would call her wardrobe. Luckily, this was the kind of hole-in-the-wall diner that wouldn't care. Hey, it was Nevada. They'd all seen weirder stuff.

Taylor's chuckle was a deep, rich sound. "I was asking about how the show hosting thing was going, but that's not going to make Andi Manning blush. 'Fess up. What's got you pink in the cheeks?"

So many things. All of which involved Dean's hands, Dean's lips, Dean's erection sliding into her body. She crossed her legs to suppress the sudden throb between them. "The hosting thing is going great. It's only been two days, but it's not bad. The clothes suck, but otherwise it's...great."

"Uh-huh, that's...great." The other woman tapped her fingers against the laminated menu in front of her. "Tell me what's really going on. Come now, you can tell old Auntie Taylor anything."

Snorting, Andi rolled her eyes. *Old*, ha. Taylor's red curls were cropped short, and even in her firefighter's uniform, she looked fresh and pretty. "Please, passing your thirtieth birthday doesn't qualify you for Social Security."

The two of them had been friends for years, bonding over their shared love of bad horror movies, being a woman in a line of work overwhelmingly populated by men, and having boyish first names, thanks to fathers who'd wanted sons but had daughters instead. In fact, Taylor had the *same* name as her dad. And both of them had followed in their father's footsteps professionally, so usually they understood where the other was coming from.

Taylor wrinkled her nose. "I feel as dried up as someone ready for Social Security. If I don't get laid again soon, my hymen's going to grow back."

A crack of laughter spilled out of Andi. "That would be tragic, yes."

Her friend flicked back her curls. "You're telling me. So…"

"So…" Damn that blush, damn those memories that had been giving her hot flashes all day. She hated it. She loved it. She didn't know what she felt, or what she was going to do about it when she figured it out. "I sort of ended my own dry spell. With Dean Kasen."

The announcement was greeted by a long moment of silence. When Andi looked up, her best friend's eyes and mouth formed three perfect circles of shock. Taylor sputtered, but didn't get a chance to finish the thought when a waitress approached their table. "What can I get you ladies?"

"Cheeseburger, medium rare. Root beer and French fries with that, thanks." Taylor all but shoved her menu into the waitress's arms.

"I'll have the club sandwich with fries and a Sprite." Andi handed her menu over as well, and they waited until they were alone again.

"Okay." Turning bright blue eyes on her, Taylor's expression grew serious. "First, was it good? Second, are you okay with shagging your boss? Third, holy crap, he's hot. Way to end the drought."

Andi rolled her eyes. "It hasn't been *that* long!"

"Oh, yes, it really has." The redhead made a face. "I'm working on eighteen months, and you had me beat."

"Okay, so maybe it's been a while." She didn't do random hookups, and she hadn't met anyone who sparked her interest in a while. Then again, she'd randomly hooked up with her boss. And liked it. A lot. Jesus, she was a hot mess.

"Uh-huh." Taylor winked and sat back as the waitress brought their drinks.

Andi stuck a straw in her soda, a little smile curling her lips when she remembered everything she'd done with Dean the night before. They'd given his desk a real workout. She shut those thoughts down.

Hot. Mess. Very, very hot.

"Well, the look on your face gives me the answer to my first question."

"Yeah, it was good." She sighed. "I don't know if I'm okay with shagging the garage owner, but it's a little late now, isn't it? Besides, I don't even know if he wants to keep doing what we did last night. It could have been a one-time itch he scratched."

"Would you be okay with that?"

Would she? "It would be easier that way, but...I don't know. I never thought we'd go there. Sure, I fantasized about going there, but I didn't think we ever *would*. He's my boss, and I love my job."

But why did the bottom drop out of her stomach when she even considered last night being a one-night stand? She realized that *she* was the one who'd fantasized, not Dean. It meant more to her than it did to him. Partially, it was that she wasn't usually a one-night wonder. It wasn't her style. Partially, it was that it had been *amazing*, and who wouldn't want another big helping of amazing? There was more to it than that, but she wasn't ready to try to define it. Everything in her shied away from doing so, so for once in her life, she chickened out on confronting a problem.

Taylor took a sip of her drink, her gaze pinning Andi in place. "That does complicate things."

"Oh, yeah." She let a wider grin cross her face, though her emotions were still writhing in jumbled confusion. "But, it was fantastic anyway."

The corners of her friend's eyes crinkled. "Well, if you're going to end up hip-deep in complicated, you might as well get your O-face on in the process, right? Just to make it worth it."

"You said it." But had it really been worth it? Would it have been better to have never known for sure how good it was to live out her longest-running fantasy? She hadn't craved anything as much as she'd craved Dean Kasen since she'd saved for three years as a teen to buy her first classic Camaro. There'd never been another flesh-and-blood man who'd come close to Dean, and that was utterly terrifying. She wanted more, and she wanted to run like hell.

She didn't know what she wanted, and that was the most terrifying thing of all.

Chapter 3

Jesus, he needed coffee. A gallon of it. And it was just his luck that he'd run out at home and forgotten to buy more. No, not luck. Distraction. He'd meant to pick some up on the way home from the shop yesterday, but he'd gotten sidetracked by banging Andi's brains out.

Grit burned his eyes as he shut and locked his front door, jogging down the street toward a nearby restaurant he preferred. He'd already called in his order, so with any luck it would be ready to go by the time he got there. Good food and just down the block. He couldn't beat that. After the long haul from Reno to Sacramento and back again, he just wasn't up to dealing with a drive to the grocery store. Some take-out food and a to-go cup of java and he'd be set for the evening.

Maybe after a good night of sleep, he'd know what he was going to say to Andi when he got to the shop in the morning. After a day of wrestling with the problem, he still didn't have a clue. He'd dodged a bullet by having to pick up the new VW engine, but that reprieve was dwindling fast. Should he act like nothing had happened? Should he go through with asking her to bow out as host just so he could go back to keeping his hands to himself? Hell, he'd never slept with an employee, and with good reason. What should his next move be? It was unsettling that he didn't know. He liked to be in control, he liked to have his head on straight and a plan in place. Right now? He was just twisting in the wind.

It was a nasty shock when he walked into *his* restaurant and saw Andi there, eating dinner with another woman. Even then, he couldn't stop the punch of lust that reverberated through him. Last night should have slaked his need for her, but instead it had intensified. His body went rock-hard at the first glance, his fingers itching with the desire to touch her. It didn't help that she clearly hadn't changed after work, because this outfit was just as revealing as the one she'd worn the day before. God help him.

The two women's conversation died when they noticed him standing in the doorway. He cleared his throat, moving forward until he stood next to their table. "Hi, Andi."

Wow, smooth opening line, Kasen. He managed not to wince at his own banality. Barely. Both women stood to face him, Andi silent and wearing an inscrutable expression, the leggy redhead with her staring with open curiosity.

She grinned, eyeing him up and down before she held out her hand. "I'm Taylor Vance, Andi's best friend. Nice to meet you."

"And you." He gave her hand a quick shake and let it go. "I didn't mean to interrupt. I was just stopping in to grab a take-out order."

"You're not interrupting, actually. We just finished, and I have to head over to the firehouse for my shift." She gestured to the crisp uniform she had on. The redhead laid some cash on the table, turned, and gave Andi a quick hug. "Call me later, okay?"

"I will."

And then he had Andi all to himself. He stared at her for a long moment, unsure what to say. He'd known her for years, spoke to her every day at work, but last night had thrown the universe out of whack. What were they now? Employee and boss? Lovers? All of the above? Hell if he knew. "Are you all right? About what happened?"

Her cheeks pinkened and she glanced around. "Um, do we have to talk about this here?"

"No, let me pick up my order. Then we can take a walk and talk."

"Okay." Her breath sighed out, and relief relaxed her features.

He paid for his food at the counter, picked up the plastic bag and Styrofoam cup of coffee, and turned to head out with Andi close on his heels. He transferred everything to one hand so he could hold the door open for her, and then set his palm on her lower back to steer her in the right direction. She shivered and glanced over her shoulder at him but didn't pull away. That hot spark of awareness flashed in her gaze, and his insides tightened as he fought the need to reach for her. His shaft went harder than steel, making his jeans uncomfortably tight. He spread his fingers wider on her back, his pinky edging under the hem of her T-shirt. "Just around the corner here."

"Where are we going?" she asked when they hit the sidewalk beyond the small parking lot.

"My place. I live just down the street." A warning sounded in the back of his mind, telling him this was not a good idea, that testing his control this soon after losing it entirely was a bad plan. He ignored that inner voice and kept his hand right where it was on her back, urging her on. "You wanted to talk in private, didn't you?"

She hesitated, but then her chin dipped in a nod and she kept walking. The silence was only punctuated by their footsteps on the sidewalk. She cleared her throat. "Um...I didn't know you lived around here."

Humming in his throat, he traced his finger along the top of her tight cut-off jeans. "Most of my life. I bought the place from my parents when they decided to retire to Phoenix."

"Wow." She stopped in the driveway, arching her eyebrows. "This house looks a lot newer than anything your parents could have owned."

He shrugged and urged her forward again. "I've updated a bit since I bought it."

"A bit, huh? Yeah, right." She jogged up the porch steps. "What do your parents think?"

"I warned them I was going to make changes when I bought the house." He hated to stop touching her, but he had to dig into his pocket for his keys to unlock and open the front door. Though he was glad that the awkwardness seemed to have abated a bit. "My mom loves it. Dad was grumpy about it for a while, but that was more about his doctor making him retire than anything about the house. They come stay with me a few times a year. Dad even helps me out with some of the projects now."

She chuckled as she stepped inside the house. "Sounds like your dad. And mine. Can't keep a tool out of their hands."

"Sounds like us, too."

"Yeah, it does. I'm happiest with a wrench in my hand and a car that needs a fix."

"I know. I like that about you." A foolish thing to say, but true nonetheless. She really *got* the way he enjoyed getting a little dirty working on a car. It felt good when he brought one of those old beauties back to life.

A surprised smile fluttered at the corners of her mouth before she spun away and waved an arm around to encompass the house. "Uh, okay. Um...I've never done much in the way of home renovation. What projects are you doing that your father helps with?"

Equal parts relief and disappointment filled him that she'd ignored his personal comment. "Most of the big stuff is done. I'm installing some built-in bookshelves in the office, but that's about it."

"The place is beautiful. You've done a great job with it."

Warmth filled him at the compliment. He'd had several people make flattering comments about his house, but none of them got to him the way hers did. He *wanted* her to like his place, and he wanted her approval. It shouldn't matter what she thought, but it did. Forcing himself to follow her example and sidestep the personal, he led the way into the kitchen to set his food and coffee on the counter. He popped the top off of the Styrofoam cup. "You want half of this?"

"No, thanks. Caffeine too late in the day keeps me up all night, and I need some sleep after—" She cut herself off, but it was too late.

"After we screwed like minks most of the night last night?" On the desk, in his office chair, against the wall. For hours. He hadn't been able to get enough, and it was a lot more fun than facing the conversation they were about to have now.

Dragging in a breath that made her breasts threaten to spill from her shirt and made his erection chafe against his fly, she sighed. "Eat your dinner—we can talk about what happened afterward."

Sounded good to him, so he dug into his food. Not only because he was hungry, but because he wouldn't mind getting a few more minutes before he had to end something that had never really had a chance to begin.

There were times when he really hated the sense of responsibility his parents had drilled into his head. This was definitely one of those times.

Chapter 4

Andi cleared her throat and cast around for something—any-thing—to say that would stop the words *screwed like minks* from repeating in her head and reminding her body of how much she'd enjoyed every second of getting naked with Dean. "Um…I was thinking we might go for some whitewall tires on the Bug. It might add an old-school flare to the car without a lot of added expense."

He met her glance, his gaze considering. "That might look nice with this one. The owner seems to really want a retro look. Good idea. We can run it by the guys in the morning."

"Great." It *was* great. She actually got to have a say in things now. She could make suggestions before, but now people would know it was her idea because they'd see her talking about it on the show. Pride suffused through her, and she grinned.

Smiling back at her, he leaned forward and she got a deep whiff of the light cologne he wore. God, he smelled good. "Okay, so, no coffee for you. Did you want something else?"

Oh, yeah, she wanted something. Heat rolled through her in a wave that centered between her thighs. But he was her boss. Last night had been an impulse, spontaneous combustion, but she had no excuses now. A tiny part of her wished she didn't have to have any excuses, that she could just jump him and forget the consequences.

If he even wanted to keep doing this. Her. Whatever. Dean was tough to read at the best of times, and her own jumbled emotions didn't make it easier to discern his. He was still staring at her, an eyebrow raised. Right. He'd asked her a question.

"Water," she blurted. "Ice water, please."

Something to cool her down, that was the ticket.

He gave her an odd look but set his fork down and went to fetch her some water from his refrigerator. The thing was stainless steel and as polished as the rest of the house. It was obvious a lot of hours had gone in to remodeling. She'd had no idea that he'd done anything like this outside of work. Dean was the quieter of the two Kasen cousins, and she was pretty sure Jesse spent his time away from the garage bouncing from one bed to another. Somehow, she'd imagined Dean doing the same...and just never mentioning it. The truth made him even more attractive, and that was a dangerous thought, because she was already far too attracted to him.

A glass frosted with condensation landed on the counter in front of her, and she startled. When she looked up, Dean's gaze was warm with understanding. "This is a little weird for me too. Try to relax."

"I'll do my best, but I can't promise anything." She took a sip from the water while he sat down in front of his dinner.

"Fair enough." Picking up his fork, he scooped up a bite of the meatloaf and mashed potatoes he'd brought home. "If you don't want to watch me eat, you can give yourself a tour."

Well, that showed more trust than she would have expected. "Nothing here you don't want me to see?"

"I don't keep skeletons in my closets."

No, he was a straight shooter, always had been. That was one of the things she liked about him, both personally and professionally. Having a boss who was genuine, decent, and didn't jerk people around was refreshing, particularly as the only woman at Kasen's Kustom. It was also one of the many reasons she'd wanted to jump his bones for so long.

Yep, her thoughts were determined to circle back around to the sexy times. Maybe a self-guided tour wasn't such a bad idea. Turning away, she headed down the hall. There was an office, which was clearly being prepped for installing the bookshelves he'd mentioned, a small powder room, two guest bedrooms with a Jack-and-Jill bathroom in between, and then the master at the end of the hall. She only gave a quick peek in there, because knowing what his bedroom looked like wasn't going to help quell her fantasies at night. Details like that would just make them more concrete.

The entire house was undeniably masculine, in blues and grays with cedar and brushed nickel accents, but it was still comfortable. Homey. Somehow, she'd always pictured him in a bachelor pad, maybe an upscale version of a college dorm. As had been the case so far, she far preferred the reality to her fantasy, and that was dangerous.

Wandering back into the main living area, she found him still eating, so she asked, "Which way is the garage?"

She was a mechanic. Of course, she wanted to check out his garage.

The corners of his eyes crinkled in a grin, but since his mouth was full of food, he silently pointed to a door on the opposite side of the room.

She smiled in return, strode over, and slipped out into the darkened space. The familiar scent of motor oil hit her as she blindly reached for the wall beside the door, flipping on the light. His gleaming green 1969 Chrysler 300 held pride of place in the middle of the garage, with shelves and toolboxes lining the perimeter. She walked around the car, noting the construction supplies on the shelves. Spare cans of the blue and gray paints she'd noted inside, plus paint trays, brushes, and rollers. She ran her fingers along the drawer of a large red toolbox, which looked much like those at the Kasen's Kustom garage.

The door to the house opened and Dean stood there, propping one forearm against the doorjamb. "Does it all pass inspection, Ms. Manning?"

She huffed out a laugh. "Your house is lovely, which I didn't necessarily expect. Your garage, on the other hand, is anal retentively organized, which is exactly what I would have expected from you."

"Was that an insult or a compliment?"

"A little of both." She dipped one shoulder in an unapologetic shrug.

The side of his mouth kicked up in a half-smile, and there was something wicked that sparked in his gaze. Need tightened her insides, and just that easily she wanted him again with a desperation that left her breathless.

She shook her head at herself. "What are we doing, Dean?"

"I honestly don't know." He straightened away from the doorjamb, waving her back into the house.

When she stood in his living room again, she sighed and met his gaze squarely. "I just never thought...I mean, we work together. I work *for* you."

There. One of them was bound to say it, so she might as well get it out in the open.

He nodded. "I'm struggling with that one myself."

Running his hands through his hair, he left it standing in dark furrows. His brows drew together, but he huffed out a laugh and shook his head ruefully.

Yeah, that was a sentiment she could relate to. "This whole thing was just…"

"Not like me at all," he finished for her. "My dad would beat me senseless for hooking up with an employee of the garage. That's not how to run a business, and he'd say he taught me better. Not only that, but my hookup was *in the office*." His eyes darkened and a muscle flexed in his jaw. "But I don't regret it, which my old man would also kill me for. Hell, I'd kill Jesse or any of the other guys if I found out they did what I did, and I *still* don't regret it. You were a walking wet dream in that sexy getup, and being close to you just made me explode. The sex was amazing, no matter how stupid or unprofessional."

Wincing a little, she brushed a hand down her equally revealing outfit. It stung that the thing to push him over the edge was the tarted-up version of her, which wasn't her at all, but she lifted her chin. Okay, so it was just hot sex. She was an adult, she could handle that. It wasn't her usual arrangement, but whatever. "So, what do we do now? Pretend nothing happened?"

"Is that what you want?" His gaze bored into her, demanding the truth, demanding answers she didn't know if she could give.

Her stomach clenched and she balled her fingers into fists to still their sudden shaking. "I want…I don't know what I want. I want more of you, I want things to work out at the garage with the show, but I don't know if it's possible to have both. What do you want?"

A short laugh cracked from him. "Basically the same thing you want, but I don't know if it's possible either. I don't like mixing business with personal—I think it's a bad plan that'll blow up in our faces. Hell, I was going to ask you to step back from the show and just go back to how things were before, but the longer I think about it, the more I think that wouldn't solve anything. It would cause more problems...between us, with the garage, with the show, with the new producer. And it just wouldn't be fair to you, would it? You like doing the show—I can see it on your face." He sighed and rubbed a hand over the back of his neck. "We can't close the barn door after the horse is out, or however that saying goes."

"Where does that leave us?" After that recitation, it took everything in her to ask the question, but she had to know.

A self-deprecating smile twisted up the corners of his lips. "I want you. Again. That's where it leaves us. I've been going around and around with it in my head, and I can't get past that one simple fact. I want you. I burn for you. I can't imagine looking at you all day, every day and not touching you."

Molten heat poured through her body at his words. If a twinge of disappointment shot through her that it was so obviously a physical thing for him, she ignored it. She'd been lusting after *his* sexy bod for years, and now she had the chance to have a wild fling with him. It was enough. It had to be, didn't it? "So, you've decided you like what you see and now you want us to have a casual, no-strings affair that doesn't mess with our professional lives. Do I have that right?"

Shadows moved behind his eyes and his mouth worked for a long moment before he spoke. "Yes. I like what I see. I want to see more of it until one or both of us decide to end things. Once that happens, we walk away, no harm, no foul."

She was insane. She had to be, because she was actually going to do this. Have an affair with her boss. Not just a heat of the moment decision, but with her eyes wide open and her brain engaged. The breath eased out of her lungs. Just sex...she could do this. It helped that he clearly only wanted to sleep with her because of her new makeover.

Fine. It was better this way, less messy. She got to end her dry spell in a really awesome way, and he got to keep scratching this sudden itch he had. The justifications rang a little hollowly, but she pushed that aside. If she could have more of him, she wanted to.

The decision made, she met his gaze. "Okay. I'm in for as long as this lasts."

"Good." His pupils dilated, lust tightening his features. "Take your clothes off."

The heat sluicing through her exploded into something wild, uncontrollable. She shuddered, some muscles tightening, others loosening as her body readied itself for sex. Stepping away from the counter, she tugged at the bottom of her shirt and pulled it over her head. His gaze zeroed in on her breasts, where a clear outline of her nipples showed through her thin cotton bra. Anticipation gripped her, and her legs shook as she reached down to pop open the button on her very short cut-off jeans.

He drew in a sharp breath as the tight denim took her panties down with them while she worked her shorts off. She'd never stripped like this for a man before, been naked while he watched, fully dressed. It was erotic, made her burn even hotter. Kicking her heels off, she stepped out of the jean shorts and stood in nothing but her bra. Hunger showed in his gaze as he perused every inch of her.

"Come here." His voice was low and tight, almost a growl.

She moved within his reach, and he wrapped a brawny arm around her waist to haul her forward. The feel of his hard body against hers just ratcheted her excitement up even more. She struggled to pull the back of his shirt out of the waistband of his pants. "I need to touch you."

"Yes." He released her, shedding his clothes in moments, though his eyes never left her. "I want you naked. Everything off."

Arching an eyebrow, she flicked open the front closure on her bra and let gravity peel it away from her breasts. She shrugged and let it drop to the floor with the rest of her clothes. "You have a tattoo."

Something else she hadn't known about him until the night before when she'd seen him nude for the first time. He was a beautiful man, all brown skin, dark hair, and piercing green eyes. Every inch of him was sculpted muscle. Broad shoulders sloped down to heavy pecs, hard abs, the most luscious butt she'd ever had her hands on, and long, hard legs. Around one thigh was a wide black band of tattooing.

He grunted. "A lot of guys have tats. Jesse's got them all over his back. Sanchez is covered in them."

"I know. Even I have one." She pointed to the lotus blossom on her hip.

"I noticed. It's sexy." He bent forward and kissed the small flower, and she shivered.

"But that one looks tribal. Does it mean anything, or did you just walk into the tattoo parlor and point to something on the wall?"

"Uh-huh, that sounds like me." He snorted, nipping at the skin below her tattoo. "No, it means something. I'm a quarter Hawaiian—my mother's mother—and when I was eighteen, I went over and had a traditional thigh band done. They tap the ink into the skin rather than use a tattoo gun. Hurt like hell, but it was important to me to do it right. Since it's permanent, I didn't want something stupid I'd regret later."

"That's not something a lot of teens would consider." But it showed he was always as much in control as he was now. Serious and cautious.

He shrugged, his words confirming her thoughts. "I don't make permanent choices lightly, never have." Glancing up at her, a quick grin flashed across his face. "Enough talking."

His fingers skimmed her hips, her waist, up her ribs to her breasts. The breath stopped in her lungs, and her body arched into his hands. She swallowed. "Yeah, enough talking."

Figuring turnabout was fair play, she splayed her hands on his chest, her fingers brushing over his nipples. He shuddered, a low groan wrenching from him. A wicked grin curled her lips, and she let her tongue slide along them, knowing he'd watch.

As expected, his gaze zeroed in on her mouth. "I want to kiss you."

"Where?" She offered up the question with a cheeky grin.

He brushed the pad of his thumb over her lower lip. "I'd start here." His other hand rose to curve around the side of her neck, his fingers caressing her skin. "Then here." Both palms slipped lower until he cupped her breasts, his thumbs circling her nipples until they drew into aching points of need. "Definitely here." He skimmed his fingertips down her midriff, over the soft swell of her belly, and down to the juncture of her thighs. "And I'd like to take my sweet time kissing you right here."

Yes. Her breath shallowed to nothingness at the very thought of him going down on her. She wanted that so much. Her heart pounded so loudly in her ears, it drowned out all other sounds. Goose bumps broke down her limbs when his fingers teased the thatch of hair between her legs.

"What do you say, Andi?" Eyebrows arching, he leaned away to look at her face.

She had to clear her throat twice to get words out. "I'm game."

"Excellent. I think this calls for a change of venue." With that, he bent down and scooped her into his arms.

A squeak emerged from her mouth, and she clutched at his shoulders, which made him laugh as he walked down the hall. In under a minute he set her back on her feet next to a big bed. His bed.

He curled one brawny arm around her waist and pulled her flush against his naked form. Her softness molded to his harder angles, and the sensation made her moan. He caught the sound with his mouth, kissing her with a thoroughness that turned her insides to molten lava. She met his tongue with hers, giving as good as she got. Their breathing went ragged, their hands sliding over each other's bodies, attempting to touch every inch of skin they could reach.

He backed her toward the bed, his lips never leaving hers as he lowered her to the mattress. His weight pressed her into the soft comforter, the crisp hair on his chest rubbing against her nipples as they moved together. Propping himself on his elbows above her, he kissed his way along her jaw, nipped at her earlobe, and moved down to nip and suck the sensitive tendon that connected her throat to her shoulder.

She rolled her head on the mattress, arching her neck to give him freer access. "That feels so good, Dean."

"So, I'm doing this right?" His voice was a low rumble against her skin, and he trailed his tongue along her collarbone.

"*Very* right." She moaned when he reached her breasts and took her nipple into his mouth, sucking lightly and then biting down. The pleasure-pain sent a lightning strike of need from breast to loin, and she writhed under him. He turned his attention to the other nipple, treating it to the same sweet torment. Her sex clenched on emptiness with each pull of his lips on the tight peak. The intensity was more than she could bear, and she raked her short nails up his back. "More, please. I need more. I need you."

A great shudder wracked his body at her words, and his lips grazed her midriff as he moved down to settle between her thighs. His broad shoulders forced her legs wide, exposing her to his gaze. She was too far gone to be embarrassed that he looked his fill, and she arched her hips toward him in shameless abandon.

He blew a stream of cool air against her slick, overheated skin. "Is this what you want, honey?"

"God, yes." She choked on a breath, hot shivers running through her. "I want you to do exactly what you said and...take your sweet time kissing me right there."

A pleased hum escaped him before he dove in to feast on her wet flesh. The first touch of his tongue made her gasp, and she reached down to bury her hands in his hair, holding him close. Nothing, *nothing*, had prepared her for what it would be like to have Dean Kasen use his lips and teeth and tongue to pleasure her. Time seemed to stretch out and become elastic as she fell into a place that was pure sensation. Her entire world narrowed to what he was doing to her and how very fine it made her feel.

He sank two fingers deep inside her and lifted his head for a moment. "Do you like this, Andi?"

"I like it so much. Don't stop, *please*." The low whimper of her voice stunned her. Had she ever sounded so needy in her life?

He formed his lips around her nub and sucked hard. Her body arched in shock, and wanton pleasure sizzled along her nerves. He gave his fingers an expert twist that rubbed over just the right spot inside her and made her mewl in utter want. Her inner muscles clenched around his thick digits, the first quivers of completion beginning to build within her. It wouldn't be long before she came apart for him. He worked her swiftly with his mouth and hand, pushing her to the very edge of her endurance. His lips drew hard on her sensitive nub again and she broke. A sob ripped from her as white-hot ecstasy burst in her, so sharp she cried out as her orgasm hit her with the force of a tsunami.

Climax still pulsed through her when he pushed himself upright.

He lunged for his nightstand, and she heard him tearing open a condom wrapper. Moments later, he was over her, pulling her ankles onto his shoulders, sliding his hands down her legs to lift her hips.

"Hurry," she demanded. Even though she'd just come, she wanted everything he had to give her, and she wanted it now. Right now. "I want you inside me."

"So demanding," he chided, though the roughness of his movement and wildness in his gaze told her he wasn't going to be able to wait much longer either. Rubbing the head of his erection up and down her slit, he positioned himself at her opening and pressed into her. She was already so slick, he was soon hilted within her, and the stretch was pure heaven.

"Dean." Her fingers curled into the sheets beneath her, and she wriggled to press herself even closer to him. "You have no idea how good this feels."

"I think I have an idea." His lips curved in a tight smile. A flush ran under his skin, and sweat slid down from his temples, beaded his chest. The rough hair at his groin rasped against her backside as he seated himself inside her. He filled her to the limit, and the sensation was more than she knew how to handle, so she gave herself over to it. There was no choice, there was only this moment with a man she wanted more than her next breath.

The rhythm he set for them was as hard and fast as she craved, and her hands balled in the sheets. Excitement writhed like a living thing within her, and she knew she wouldn't last long. She loved feeling him move inside her, loved the smells and sounds of sex that filled the bedroom. Yes. God, yes. He bored down on her, taking her hard, but he moved his fingers around to tease her slick flesh. Nothing else would have catapulted her over the edge again so fast, and she came, screaming his name. Her thighs jerked against his shoulders, her hips rising to meet his swift thrusts. Her sex clenched on his thick shaft, and the flex and release went on forever as orgasm rocketed through her.

He threw his head back as his hips hammered forward, low groans wrenching from him. His thrusts became shorter, rougher, and then he stilled and shuddered as climax dragged him under. He slumped over her, his green eyes glassy. He looked as stunned as she felt, blown away by what they'd done, by how good it felt. Her heart squeezed so tight, it stopped her breath. As terrifying as the truth was, she knew that nothing had ever been so good or so right in her entire life.

It couldn't last. Something like this was a once in a lifetime experience, like watching a comet shoot across the night sky. It burned too hot and fast to hold on to for long. She just had to enjoy the thrill while she could.

A tear slid unchecked down her cheek, and she turned her face into the mattress so he wouldn't see.

Chapter 5

Dean's biceps flexed right in front of her face, and Andi wanted to run her tongue along those thick muscles. Unfortunately, there was a garage full of men working on various parts of the car and a cameraman was wedged into the mix with them, recording every movement she and Dean made. They were trying to get the new dashboard they'd designed installed on the little VW Bug, and even though there were no seats in the car at the moment, they were still in tight quarters. Moisture slid in beads down her skin; she was upside down on the floor of the passenger side, the oversized mechanic's shirt they'd turned into a belted dress tucked around her thighs for modesty's sake. Her heel was jammed against the metal bar that would eventually hold the backseat as she strained to hold the dash up for Dean to screw it in place. The dash bobbled as he slammed his hand against something that sounded painful. "Shit, piss, mother-fucking piece of crap."

She glanced up at the camera and winked. "Sweat and swearing...it's how the real work gets done on *Revved Up*."

A chuckle rumbled from Dean and he shot her a quick grin. Another thirty seconds and he had the dashboard secured. Sighing, Andi relaxed for the first time in hours.

"That was great." Lola peeked in over her cameraman's shoulder. "What are y'all going to work on next?"

Dean swiped a hand down his face and looked into the camera as he answered. "Now that we've got the dash in, Sanchez is going to install the sound system." He motioned to an open hole in the console. "He'll wire it to the speakers throughout the car, and when he's done, we'll set Jesse loose on finishing the custom interior."

At this point, they had it down pat that when Lola asked something, they needed to basically repeat the question in the answer for a better sound bite. They had to pretend the producer wasn't there asking them anything, and instead have a natural conversation with the piece of equipment attached to the cameraman's shoulder.

Lola and her crew turned to speak to Sanchez, who hovered outside, impatient to start on his new system. Most of their crew had tattoos, but Sanchez took it to the next level. He was tattooed from his bald head down to his feet—every visible inch of skin was covered in black ink. That didn't affect his amazing gift for car electronics, which made each overhaul unique.

Andi took the opportunity to pull herself upright and out of the car without accidentally flashing the camera. She kept one hand on the hem of her dress to keep it down.

"What are you wearing under that thing?" Dean's voice was a silken whisper in her ear, and she tensed.

Lust sparked inside her, but so did pain. Jesus, she couldn't take much more of this, being his sex toy. She'd thought she could do an affair, but after two weeks, she just wanted to crawl out of her own skin. Even telling herself it was just sex hadn't kept her from wishing for more. She'd invited him to hang out at her place a couple of times to see if he wanted to get to know her better outside of work. He'd turned her down, crushing what little hope she'd had. Tears pricked her eyes. This wasn't her. The sexy clothes, the no-strings shagging. She just...couldn't. She loved the show and the sex, but she hated herself for going along with both. This had to stop before she turned into someone she didn't respect anymore.

Dean watched emotions shift across Andi's face.

"We need to talk." Her voice was soft, but those were words that would send a chill down anyone's spine.

His muscles went taut. "Do we?"

"Yes. We do. After work is probably best." She nodded and spun on a heel, tripping over her stilettos while she jerked at her painted-on clothes.

She wasn't happy, that much was clear. The deeper they'd gotten into their affair, the more shadows had lurked in her gaze each time he touched her. It had been two weeks, and he could feel a time bomb ticking down on how long he had left with her. His gut twisted painfully. He didn't want it to end, but she wasn't the type for a short-term fling. He'd known that about her all along, but it was all he could offer. To make things solid, permanent, just wasn't possible. It would mix business and personal far too much. An affair with his employee was already too stupid to mention, but an actual relationship? Disaster. He couldn't do it. Things had spun too far out of control as it was, and he was barely hanging on.

The hours until the end of the workday ground by in slow, agonizing procession. He sat in his office, forcing himself to close the books for the month, but his mind kept straying to Andi. This was it. This was the end. A band of emotion he couldn't begin to name wrapped tight around his chest. The garage had cleared out, but he knew she was still here. He'd explode out of his skin if he sat and waited for her, so he shoved to his feet and went to hunt her down.

He found her standing next to the VW, her head down.

"We did well on this one. It's almost done." She ran a reverent hand over the side of the car, and he stared, wishing like hell it was his skin her fingers stroked.

"Yeah, the car's going to be great." The car was the only thing that would be great. Dread pressed down on him, an ugly darkness that seeped into his flesh.

"Okay." She finally met his gaze, sadness and determination swimming in their hazel depths. Her mouth set in a firm line. "I need to talk to you about some stuff."

He didn't want to hear it, couldn't stand the thought of her walking away from him. Crowding her against the side of the car, he slammed his mouth over hers, cutting off anything she might have said. One last taste. He had to have it, her. Just one last time. She didn't resist but twined her arms around his neck and threw herself into the kiss with a ferocity that stunned him. She bit his lower lip, then thrust her tongue between his lips. They fought for control, biting, sucking, and licking.

His fingers fumbled for the buttons on her shirtdress, but after a few seconds, he gave up and just ripped the top open. He heard the clatter of buttons hitting the concrete floor, but he ignored it and slid his hand in to cup her pert breast. Scraping his thumbnail over her nipple through her bra made her moan into his mouth, made his blood race in his veins. Her hands moved down to his fly, working open the tab and zipper. His shaft lengthened, throbbed with the need to be inside her welcoming warmth. Urgency screamed through him, as if any second might be his last, as if he needed to brand her essence into his mind while he still had the chance.

Dropping his palms to her thighs, he slid up to the curve of her butt under her dress. Cotton underwear, as usual. He tried to chuckle, but it almost emerged a rough sob. He shoved back the emotion that roiled within him, focusing on the physical as he'd done for the last two weeks. Hooking his thumbs in the top of her panties, he dragged them down and let them fall to the floor. She pulled his erection free of his jeans, and he had to be inside her. Reaching blindly for his wallet and the condom inside of it, he mated his tongue with hers, unwilling to lose the taste of her for even a second. Then the foil packet was in his hand, but she took it from him, tore it open and sheathed him. Jesus, she was perfect, the closest to heaven he'd ever know.

Grasping her smooth backside, he jerked her off her feet and her legs cinched around his hips. The head of his erection slid along her wet slit. So close to where he wanted to be. Lifting her higher, he pushed her back against the car and used her position for leverage to impale her on his shaft. A whimper burst from her throat, and he couldn't stop a groan. She bit his lip, but it only drove him onward, the slight pain accentuating his pleasure. This was good. So good. The slickness of her made him burn, pushed him to the edge of madness. He pulled out, the drag of her flesh around his erection pure eroticism.

She broke her mouth away from him and threw her head back. "Hurry, Dean."

Her voice was as desperate as he felt, driven by the need to push away the inevitable for just a few more minutes. One swift thrust and he was back inside her, riding her hard against the side of the VW, her head bowed backward over the top of the vehicle. He opened his mouth on her exposed throat, sucking and biting as he thrust into her. She clenched her channel around his shaft, squeezed his waist with her legs as she moved with him, took him deeper. His muscles drew tighter as he fought back the need to come. His hips bucked as he rammed into her as hard as he could, *needing* more, but knowing he'd never have more than this.

That band of emotion closed around his chest again, and he moved faster, tried to outrun it. Sweat slid down his face, his lungs heaving as he fought for air, but each breath brought the scent of her and him and sex. The echo of skin slapping against skin ricocheted through the garage along with their gasps and moans. The carnal cacophony just excited him, and he groaned against her throat. "Andi, Andi, Andi..."

Just her name, it was the only thought he had left. She arched in his arms, twisting as she exploded into climax. Her fingers bit into his shoulders, her legs tightening around his thrusting hips. The sweet feel of her core spasming on his shaft shoved him into orgasm. He stopped fighting, just let it roll over him in one hot wave as he jetted into her. Shudders wracked his body, and he held her closer, buried his face in her neck, and continued rocking into her until his erection began to soften. Anything to hold off reality for just a little bit longer.

Andi sobbed on a breath, pushing at his shoulders. "I'm done, Dean. I can't do this anymore."

He staggered back, letting her feet slide to the floor. "W-what?"

Even though part of him had known it was coming, his belly heaved, bile burned the back of his throat, and he had to fight the need to bend over and vomit when she said the words that would end it all.

"No more of this. No more being afraid to bend over and do my job because I might fall out of my top, no more breaking my ankles in high heels, no more shorts that ride up my butt or skirts that could pass as belts. *No more of this.* This is not what I signed on for. This is not who I am." She curled her fingers into the torn fabric of her shirt and blinked back tears, her voice giving a betraying crack that made his heart clench in his chest. "I can't play this part anymore. I can't be the girl you want, all sexy bombshell who only wants a quick lay. I thought

I could, but…I can't." Her breathing hitched on a sob she struggled to quell. "I give up. I quit. I'll bring in a resignation letter in the morning so it's official and the network can start looking for someone else."

He reached for her, hating the pain in her eyes, hating everything about this, wishing he could stop it, could make it better for her, but knowing he couldn't. "Andi—"

She cut him off, planting her lips on his and wrapping her arms tight around his neck for a short, hard kiss. Then she tore herself out of his embrace and ran for the door, slamming it behind her, the sound echoing in the empty garage.

As empty as Dean felt.

"**Y**ou're an idiot."

Dean rubbed a hand over tired eyes, not even bothering to look up as his cousin stomped into the office and parked himself behind his desk. It had been two days since Andi had been in to the garage. She'd had her friend Taylor drop off her letter of resignation. Dean didn't even want to consider the pathetic part of himself that had been hoping to see Andi one last time. But it was over, just as he'd known it would be. Instead of his no harm, no foul plan of them going on as they had before, she was just gone.

Gone.

The word punched him in the gut, pain exploding through every inch of his body. He hurt, deep down to his very soul. He'd never known anything could hurt like this, could rip into him and leave him bleeding.

"You're not even going to try to fix this, are you?" Jesse snorted.

Dean just sat there, unable to move, to think, to even breathe past the agony. She was gone. It was over. Now he just had to…live with it. Jesus Christ, he wasn't sure he could. Even before he'd touched her, Andi had been part of his life for years. He'd watched her work, seen her smile, heard her laugh and swear and just be Andi. But there would be no more of that, not anymore. Not ever again.

His cousin's chair squeaked as he swiveled around. "You know, I knew you were going to sleep with her the moment I asked her to be the show's host."

"What?" Dean dropped his hand, looking at the other man, dragging his mind away from his own misery.

"I knew you were going to sleep with her." For once, there was no teasing or laughter in Jesse's expression. "I knew the moment you had to be around her every day, all day, with no excuses to back off, you'd lose control."

"Drop dead."

"You've wanted her from the second she stepped in this shop. Before Uncle Gary even interviewed her, you were itching to have her naked. I could see it on your face. Why do you think I've never made a move on one of the sexiest women I know? Why do you think none of the other guys have? You'd have killed us."

"She's an employee of the garage." As his father had pointed out on more than one occasion. Had Jesse gotten the same warnings, or had his dad seen how Dean was drawn to her and cautioned only him?

"Not anymore. She quit, remember?"

He closed his eyes for a moment as that truth burned its way through him. "Lola's trying to talk her into coming back. Wardrobe changes."

"Ah, yeah. Lola, producer extraordinaire. Of course she'd be all over this." There was a bite to Jesse's tone. When Dean looked at his cousin again, there was a flash of some emotion on his face that Dean couldn't pinpoint. He opened his mouth to ask about what was going on there, but Jesse beat him to speech. "Andi thinks you only wanted her because of the *wardrobe changes* we made on her, right?"

"Yeah." Dean rubbed a hand over his nape.

"Because that's what you let her think."

"Yeah." He closed his eyes, hating that it was true, but knowing he'd done what he could to keep it the simple affair it should have been. It was better for everyone, though it sure as hell didn't *feel* better now.

His cousin sighed, his fingers drumming a staccato beat on his desk. "I get Lola scrambling to get Andi back on the show, but here's my question—do *you* want Andi to come back?"

Opening his eyes, Dean tried to find the right answer. "She's one of our best mechanics, she's got a gift with cars, and her ideas have been great the last couple of weeks. Why wouldn't I want her to work here?"

"Because you'd be her boss again."

"I—"

"Yeah, exactly." Jesse stabbed a finger in his direction. "Look, you're the only one who has a problem with sleeping with an employee."

"I'm sure if the guys knew, they'd think less of me. And her, which is a bigger problem." Which his dad had drilled into his head about Andi. She was a woman. She could get away with less and would have a lot tougher fight on her hands to get respect from the other men who worked in any garage. The best thing Dean could do for her was stay the hell away from her. He had. For years, he'd done exactly as his father told him, because he knew the older man was right. The last thing he'd ever want to do was hurt her.

Jesse huffed out a breath. "The guys do know. The guys also noticed her goods on display for the show. She can handle them. She *has* handled them. Do you think she'd let them get away with any kind of disrespect? No, and they know it. You don't have to save her from them."

Dean opened his mouth and closed it again, not sure what to say.

"Yeah, that's what I thought." His cousin arched an eyebrow. "Look, we don't run things exactly the same way our dads did. We have the show, right? You don't have to do everything the way your dad would have wanted. I get that workplace hookups aren't always good, but I know this isn't some game for you. You've wanted her way too long for that. Unless I miss my guess—and I haven't—you're in love with her."

In love with her. Shock reverberated through Dean, left him reeling. Yes. God, yes. He loved her. How had he missed something so huge, so right in front of his face? All the air seeped out of his lungs. "Damn."

The word sounded as stunned as he felt. What the hell was he going to do now? He hadn't lifted a finger to stop Andi from leaving, just waved her off as if all he wanted was some sexy show host. Jesus, he'd made a mess of this, and he had no one to blame but himself. He shook his head and cursed under his breath.

"Uh-huh." Jesse's grin was ripe with smugness. "So get in that pretty green Chrysler of yours, haul your sorry self over to her apartment, and tell her you like her for more than how big her tits are. Beg her to give you a chance."

"You're a pain, you know that, right?"

"You'll thank me for this in the morning. Go." His grin grew into a wicked smile. "The guys have a pool going on how long it takes you to pull your head out of your ass and get her back. I want to win, so hop to it."

Dean swallowed, ignoring the teasing. "She could turn me down flat."

"Change her mind. Convince her she loves you back."

He only wished it was as simple as his cousin made it sound. But what choice did he have? The last couple of days had been hell compared to the weeks of bliss he'd had with her in his arms. He wanted her back, he *needed* her back. At the very least, he needed to give her the truth about how he felt, which had jack to do with sexy clothes and hair and makeup. He missed her, and it might go against everything his father had taught him about how to run a business, but he wanted a chance at a real relationship, *and* he wanted her back in the garage. He'd figure out how to make the balance work. It was too important to fail now. Everything depended on it.

A life without Andi was a bleak existence.

Chapter 6

"Listen, Andi, if the wardrobe is really an issue, we can work that out. We can go for a cute tomboy look, with way more coverage. I think you're an amazing addition to the show and your chemistry with the rest of the crew is fun to watch. I'd hate to see you go because of clothing." Lola's husky voice was almost pleading, but it didn't do much to sway Andi. She deleted the voicemail message and tossed her cell phone on the couch cushion beside her.

Her phone rang, playing "Fire and Ice" by Pat Benatar. The ringtone she'd picked for Taylor. Snagging the cell, Andi tapped the button to answer. "Yeah?"

"You still wallowing in ugly clothes and sloppy hair on your couch?" The other woman's tone was wry.

Andi poked a finger through the hole in one knee of her faded yoga pants. "Yep."

"I'm giving you until Monday and then I'm coming over with a hazmat team.”

“Hey, I showered today. It’s not that bad.” Not physically anyway. Emotionally, she was a total wreck. She didn’t need to say it though. Her best friend knew. She’d seen it when she’d come over for the sobfest after Andi left Kasen’s Kustom. Taylor had insisted on taking the resignation notice in, but Andi hadn’t fought that hard. There were too many memories there, too many people who might sway her resolve to leave. Not that Dean had called or tried to keep her around. He was the only one who might change her mind and he hadn’t even attempted it. The realization broke her heart all over again. She swallowed hard, blinking to hold back tears. She cleared her throat. “I’ll start job hunting on Monday, so no need to send in a rescue squad or stage an intervention or whatever.”

Hard knocking sounded on her front door and she jolted. A prickle went down her skin. The knocking came again, but still she didn’t move. She didn’t need to look through the peephole to know who was there.

“Uh...Dean is at my door,” she whispered.

“What? No way. That jackhole has some serious balls to come around now.” Fierce protectiveness rang in her friend’s tone. “Do you want me to come over there?”

“No, I can handle this.” She thought. Maybe.

“I can hear you talking, so I know you’re in there.” Dean’s words were clear and so was the determination in his voice. “Open up, please. I don’t want to have to air our dirty laundry where your neighbors can hear.”

Crap. She didn’t even want to consider what might come out of the man’s mouth. “Taylor, let me call you back.”

Ending the call and dropping the phone on the coffee table, she walked over and pulled the door open. It hurt to see him again, stirred everything inside her into frothing madness. Her hand went white-knuckled on the doorknob.

"Can I come in? I'd rather not do this in the hall." He looked like hell, his eyes red-rimmed, the skin pinched tight around his eyes and mouth. His hands clenched and unclenched at his sides and he shifted from foot to foot. She'd never seen him like this. He was always the calm one, the one in control.

She stepped back, holding the door wide enough that they wouldn't brush against each other when he entered. It was one thing to see him for a few minutes, it was another to touch him again. She couldn't do it. Whatever fragile sense of peace she'd come to would shatter like glass. She shut the door and leaned back against it, her arms crossed over her chest. "What are you doing here?"

"I needed to talk to you, and since you quit Kasen's and *Revved Up*, that meant I had to come find you." He shoved his hands in his pockets, looking around at her apartment. "Nice place."

"You weren't very interested in seeing it before now." He'd rejected the very idea of being in her space when she'd brought it up during their two weeks together. Hell, he hadn't even wanted to hang out with her at the local bar and watch a NASCAR race. That smacked a little too much of an actual date, didn't it? It had shattered the meager hope she'd had left. Hope she'd told herself she didn't feel, but it was a lie. A lie that had grown bigger and bigger as the days had gone on until it threatened to crush her. She'd gotten to the point where she didn't even recognize herself anymore when she looked in the mirror. Who was this woman having a meaningless sexual fling, who spent every day uncomfortable and half-dressed? It wasn't her. She'd been hiding from herself, hiding how she really felt about everything. She was a mechanic, not a paid piece of eye-candy. She had real relationships, not shady affairs that she hid from the world. That wasn't what she wanted—not how she had to dress to be on the show, not how she had to act to be with Dean.

He drew in a breath and hunched his shoulders. "I was interested. I just didn't let myself act on it."

"Okay." That made no sense at all. In fact, him being here made no sense at all. "Why don't you get to the point of this visit, Dean?"

He sighed. "You think I'm just into you for the sexy clothes, right? You think that's the first time I noticed you were a woman I might want to spend some time with."

She shrugged as if it made no difference to her, but it stung like a swarm of bees. "That's how it looks from where I'm standing, yeah."

"Because that's the way I wanted it to look to you." He winced but met her gaze squarely. "I don't give a damn what you wear, Andi. I think you look just as hot right now as you do when Lola does her thing on you."

She brushed a hand down her messy ponytail and tried not to think about how ratty her clothes were. So what? This was how people dressed when they were at home. Real people didn't glam up for a night in front of the TV. "Right. I looked like a normal person all those years, and it didn't exactly have you asking me out, did it? No, it wasn't until my boobs were hanging out that you wanted a piece. Try to sell that to someone else. Are we done here?"

"Jesus, what a mess I made of this." A quiet, painful laugh escaped him. He shook his head. "I touched you because you spent the day right next to me, rubbing against me, and we were doing the damn show, so I couldn't take a break or walk away or have a breather where I reminded myself for the millionth time why I shouldn't mess around with someone whose paycheck I sign. My dad gave me that lecture, and I've given it to myself since he retired. Every single day."

"I don't understand." She shook her head, disquiet zinging through her. She wanted to back away, but she was already against the door. Why was he doing this? She'd made her decision, she'd come to grips with it. Why couldn't he just leave it at that? What happened to no harm, no foul?

He faced her, looked her dead in the eye. "I have *always* wanted you. I've always thought that you were beautiful and sexy and smart. I've always wanted the chance to be with you, and I'm not just talking about burning up the sheets. I wanted to *be with you*."

Tears glutted her eyes, and she pressed her lips together. "You could have had that. All you ever had to do was ask." She laughed, but the sound cracked in the middle. "I pretty much sold my soul the last couple of weeks for the opportunity to be with you, and it wasn't enough for you. I told you before, I can't be that girl. Whatever I am isn't what you really want. And that's okay, but let's not pretend otherwise."

"No pretending." He pulled his hands from his pockets, shook them out at his sides. "I let you think that this thing with us was all physical because I *needed* it to be just physical. I couldn't have a relationship with an employee. I focused so hard on that because I was trying not to think about..."

"About?" Her heart tripped, and she came away from the door, took a single step toward him.

"I love you." The words came out so fast, they blended together, and his face paled. His jaw clenched and his Adam's apple bobbed. "I've been avoiding admitting it to myself for so long, but when I finally let myself touch you... Jesus, I couldn't stop touching you. It scared me, because I thought I was in control for all those years and then everything was spinning out. Like, once I let go of one thing, it all came crashing in. I told myself—and you—it was just sex as a way to get a handle on where we were going, but it was too late." He spread his hands. "I'm just sorry I hurt you and pushed you away before I figured it all out."

She stared at him, uncertain what to say, what to do. Her pulse raced, her fingers trembled. She couldn't even wrap her mind around what he'd said.

But then he was talking again. "I know I don't deserve it, but I want a chance to do this right. Now that I have my head on straight."

"And now that I don't work for you, you don't have to deal with the employer issue." She didn't want to have to bring it up, but her quitting had made it a lot easier for him, hadn't it? That hurt too, that she'd walked away from a job she loved and now he suddenly wanted to be with her.

"No, I want it all, honey. I want everything. I want to share my life with you, *all* of it. I want you in the garage, on the show, in my bed every night, and in a real, honest to God, 'til death do us part kind of relationship." His lips quirked in a smile. "And for the record, yes, that was my way of telling you I want to marry you. Someday. When you're ready. I know I have a lot of ground to make up before we get to that point."

"This seems pretty sudden," she pointed out. Why was she arguing with him? Wasn't he offering her everything she could possibly want? But then, maybe that was the problem. He'd gone from offering her nothing to offering her everything. Could she really trust it? "I thought you didn't make permanent decisions lightly."

"I don't." He stepped toward her, lifting his hand to run a fingertip down her cheekbone. "I love you, Andi. I have for years. There's nothing light about this. I want permanent, and I want it with you. Just give me that chance."

His gaze was open and honest, no shadows or lies there. She could see everything he felt, and it staggered her. "I never thought you'd be interested in me. Not really. It was easier to believe you wanted the *Revved Up* version of me."

Regret darkened his eyes. "I'm sorry. I'm sorry I ever let you think you had to be someone else for me. I love you. Just you."

"I love you too." The feeling spilled out of her—she couldn't contain it anymore. It wouldn't have hurt so badly that he just wanted to sleep with her if she hadn't loved him all along. She'd never have slept with him in the first place if she didn't have feelings for him. Like him, she'd run from her emotions so long, she'd convinced herself they weren't really there. But she couldn't run forever. She'd promised when she'd left that she'd be true to herself. No more pretending. That meant being honest about how she felt and what she wanted. And she wanted to see if she and Dean could make this work. She had to try. "I'll come back to the garage and the show, but I will dress however I see fit. Lola might get me into some makeup, but that's it."

"Okay, good." His other hand rose to cup her cheek. "But what about us?"

She took a deep breath and a leap of faith. "I'm willing to give us a try too. But if we're in, I need us to be all in. No hiding it from *anyone*. We're dating, publicly. We're a couple."

He let out a huge breath she hadn't realized he was holding, and he dropped his forehead to hers. "Yes. To all of that. I'm in. All in."

A tear slipped down her cheek. Something huge and painful cracked open inside her, falling away. "I love you."

"I love you too, Andi. I'll tell you every day, I promise." His lips brushed over hers in the sweetest kiss she'd ever known. Another tear escaped, but she wrapped her arms around him, throwing herself into the contact. Yes, this was exactly what she'd wanted all along, the real thing. Intimacy, not just sex.

He bent forward and slid his arm under her knees, lifting her against his chest. Holding him tight, she kept kissing him. She'd missed him so much. The couch cushions gave under her back and he came down on top of her. She welcomed his weight on her, twined her legs around his hips and rocked herself into him. He groaned against her mouth, grinding down on her sex through their clothes. Shuddering, she pulled his shirt out of his jeans, running her hands up the smooth skin of his back, feeling the flex of muscle as he moved over her.

"Hurry, Dean," she moaned. She went hot and wet in moments, her body readying itself for his possession. It felt as if an eternity had passed since she'd had him inside her.

Rearing back, he jerked his shirt over his head while Andi sat up and removed her clothes. By the time she'd shimmied out of her pants and underwear, he was naked. He finished stripping her, tossing her yoga pants to the floor. She slid a finger up the rigid length of his erection, swirling around the head. His breathing sped, but he let her play with him.

"I want to suck you."

He shuddered and pulled her hand away, quickly covering himself in a condom. "Later. I won't last a second with your mouth on me. I want to feel you coming all around my cock."

Heat bloomed within her, growing until she was on fire. Lying back on the couch, she spread her thighs wide, letting one leg fall off the cushions. "Yes."

A chuckle rippled from him, and he guided himself to her entrance, pressing deep inside her. Her breath caught at the wonder of it, at the feeling of homecoming that rocked her to her core. This was so right, and she was done suppressing or denying the thought. This was where she belonged, where they both belonged. Together.

She grabbed his butt and arched beneath him, taking all of him. Rolling his hips, he began moving within her. The way his hard length stretched her channel was divine, and her excitement cranked up a notch. Her breath and pulse sped, sweat sealing their bodies together. The couch creaked underneath them as they ground together, faster and faster, racing each other for orgasm. His gaze met hers, dared her to look away. She could see his every emotion and she let him see hers. No more hiding anything, no more holding back. They stayed that way, locked together. He pumped into her, and her inner muscles fisted. She was so close. Her fingers curled into his back and she sobbed with the need exploding inside her.

Reaching between them, he thumbed her nub and it sent her flying. Pinpoints of light burst in her vision, and tingles broke over her limbs. Her inner muscles contracted, climax rolling over her in a wave so intense, it drowned her. She loved it, reveled in it. He rode her hard, dragging the feeling out for her, and her sex clenched each time he entered her. Throwing his head back, he shouted out his own orgasm, thrusting deep inside her once, twice, three more times before he sank down on top of her.

"I love you, Andi. Always." He buried his face in her neck and she held him close, exactly where she wanted him.

"Dean," she breathed. "I love you."

It was the deepest truth of her life. No more pretending. And that was just the way it should be.

THE END

All Tangled Up

REVVED UP, BOOK 2

C. JORDAN

CJ BOOKS

Chapter 1

Reno, Nevada

A low, throaty laugh echoed through the massive garage. The kind of sound that made a straight man's brain fog with lust. It made *Jesse's* muscles tighten with annoyance. Lola shouldn't be flaunting her hotness around his men, distracting them from their work. Kasen's Kustom Automotive was a business, damn it.

Unfortunately, it was also the set for a reality television show that overhauled classic cars, and since Lola was the show's new producer, there was nothing Jesse could do about her flirting with anyone. Normally, he loved working on the show, and he'd been thrilled when *Revved Up* had been offered national syndication, but that offer had come with Lola Adams. He glanced up from the sound system he was installing to see her flashing a smile at one of his grease monkeys.

"That's a great idea, Sanchez." Lola's voice rolled out in her slow Georgia drawl, her tone sugary sweet. She laid a hand on the tattooed man's forearm and he grinned back, leaning closer.

The two of them walked toward the car, rejoining the camera crew and mechanics who were hard at work. Eddie, one of Kasen's other employees, was bent across the hood attaching the windshield wipers, and Jesse watched his eyes glaze a bit when Lola came near. She gave Eddie a wink. "Not that we don't love your handsome face on camera, but I think we want this shot to focus on what Jesse and Sanchez are doing with the sound."

Eddie flushed when she called him handsome, and his expression conveyed how eager he was to please her. "I'll get this done in under a minute."

"I'm always impressed with the speed of this garage's crew." Her smile was charming, and combined with the form-fitting skirt and shirt made of some soft, expensive fabric, petite height and knockout curves, she was a walking wet dream. It didn't hurt that she had a face that would make Venus envious. With creamy skin, brown eyes that tilted up at the corners, and long blond hair, everything about Lola made any heterosexual man with a pulse want to reach out and touch.

"Let's just get this done," Jesse said, giving Eddie a pointed look through the windshield. The man quit staring at Lola and got his task finished as quickly as he'd promised.

"Great job," Lola complimented. Her gaze fell on Jesse and, for a split second, her grin faltered. Her gaze slid down his body, where he was sprawled half-in and half-out of the vehicle, working under the dashboard. Her perusal paused for just a moment too long on his chest and where his jeans were stretched tight over his groin. He saw the burn of desire in her gaze, felt an answering spark inside him. She jerked a bit, shook her head, and turned to Sanchez with a dazzling smile. "Are we ready for y'all to do your thing?"

Jesse barely managed to suppress a growl, forcing himself to focus on the car. If he were honest, he'd admit he was pissed off because Lola showered her attention on someone besides him. If he'd been getting more interest from her, it wouldn't matter who else she flirted with. He was clearly losing his mind. Why he even cared was beyond him. From the look of her, she'd slept her way into this job, and he had no time to babysit someone who didn't know one end of a wrench from the other. He'd been working his ass off to turn Kasen's Kustom into a force to be reckoned with, and now classic car owners from all over the world were flocking to their garage to have them work their magic in customizing those beauties. Lola was a distraction he didn't need, and it was just a shame that all he could think about when she was around was what she'd look like all tangled up in his sheets.

He snorted at his own stupidity. Yeah, he had a jones for her. She knew it too, the same way he knew she was attracted to him. But a woman like her had "high maintenance" written all over her—she was used to men giving her whatever she wanted if she so much as batted an eyelash at them. Jesse liked his women as low maintenance as possible, so for the moment, he was keeping his distance. So was she. They'd been dancing around each other since she'd arrived to start shooting the new season of *Revved Up*. Three very long months.

"Sanchez, you want to give me a hand with this?" Okay, so Jesse might not be pursuing her, but that didn't mean he wanted to watch his employees drool. Besides, sound systems were Sanchez's babies.

"Sure, boss." There was a hint of laughter in the other man's voice, but Jesse ignored it.

It took a few moments of reshuffling for the cameraman and the guy with the boom microphone to position themselves on Jesse's side of the car while Sanchez squeezed in under the steering wheel. The interior wasn't large to begin with, and Jesse was a full head taller than Sanchez, so he had to contort himself and leave his legs hanging out the open passenger door to be able to fit.

The hairs on the back of his neck rose and he knew Lola had come alongside his legs while she watched what they were doing. "So, tell us what you're going to do to this old girl today."

Dragging in a deep breath, Jesse could smell the light scent of her perfume. His body reacted, his blood heating. Damn, but she got to him. He didn't even have to look to know the shape of her breasts, the curve of her hip, the silky sheen of her pale hair. He wanted her, had since the day she'd walked into his garage.

"Boss?" Sanchez smirked. "You gonna answer the lady's question?"

Right. The other man's heavy accent made him difficult to understand on camera, so they had him talk as little as possible. Jesse sighed, climbing out of the cramped confines to let Sanchez work.

"Today, we're putting in some of the finishing touches on this 1958 Aston Martin DB Mark III, which is usually just called the Mark III. This is one of two coupe variants of the original model, the Drophead Coupe, which was more common than the Fixed Head version." Jesse leaned in to run his hand down the smooth dashboard. They'd had to reconstruct the entire interior of this one. When they'd started the overhaul, it had looked like rabid raccoons had been chewing on the seats, dash, and console for the last twenty years. "Sanchez is about done working his magic with the electronics, and then we'll put the new seats in. Done by the end of the day."

They'd painted the car baby blue with a set of bright orange racing stripes up the middle of the hood. Considering how bad a shape it had been in when it arrived, Jesse was pretty proud of the result.

He stepped out of the cameraman's way so he could get a shot of Sanchez connecting wires. When Jesse moved, he bumped into Lola, who'd also shifted positions to let her crew work. Just that innocent a touch sent heat arcing down his arm. Sweat broke out on his forehead, hot need curled in his gut, reaching down to grip his loins. He turned his head to look at her, wanting to see the passion that would spark in her gaze at times like this.

But she studiously refused to meet his eyes. She reached out to run a fingertip down the side of the sports car, a small smile curving her full lips. "She's beautiful."

"Yes. She is." But he wasn't talking about the Aston Martin.

That was when she faced him, her gaze locking with his. The moment stretched, heated. The heady smell of her hit him again, and he was close enough to feel the warmth of her body. *His* body reacted to her nearness in predictable ways. He watched her drag in a breath that lifted her breasts. So lush and lovely.

Her tongue darted out to lick her lips, and he fought a groan. "Jesse."

"What?" He edged closer, even though he knew he should back off. It was all he could do not to touch, to take. "What is it you want, Lola?"

Her brown eyes darkened, her cheeks flushing. She leaned into him until her breasts *almost* brushed his chest. "I want..."

"I think we got this shot, Lola." The cameraman cleared his throat. "Should we move on to something else?"

Shaking herself, Lola flashed an easy grin at Jesse, but avoided his gaze again. "I think Dean and Andi should be back with lunch for everyone soon. Why don't we take a break and let the guys finish up with the electronics so they can do the seats after we eat?"

Jesse shoved a hand through his hair, gripping the strands tightly. He blew out a breath. "Andi and Dean were doing that cake tasting thing for their wedding today too, so don't be surprised if they're a little late."

The food and bachelor party were the best parts of weddings, so he hoped they picked a good cake. Jesse had been roped into being his cousin's best man. It still amazed him that Dean had finally broken down and hooked up with Andi, the only female mechanic who worked for their garage. She'd also recently become the host of *Revved Up*, which Jesse had engineered to push the two together. Yep, he was a real matchmaker.

"We're not late," Andi called from the door, her brunette ponytail swinging as she walked, a huge bag from the local burger joint clutched in each hand. "Come and get it, folks!"

Just behind her was Dean, who glanced between Jesse and Lola as the blonde hurried to step away from him, tossing her hair over her shoulder. Dean arched his eyebrows and approached Jesse, pitching his tone low when he spoke. "The two of you need to just bone and get it out of your systems."

Jesse snorted. "Screw you."

"You're not my type, and screwing me wouldn't help you with your Lola problem." Dean lifted one of the drink carriers he held. "Take a drink and chill out, cousin. You're looking a little hot under the collar."

"You're right. You're not my type—I don't do douchebags." Glowering, Jesse pulled a Styrofoam cup free. "And I don't *have* a Lola problem."

His body throbbed with utter want, and his gaze kept straying to the sway of her backside as she walked away, but he was just fine otherwise.

"Denial is such a sad thing to see in a grown man. But have fun with that, douchebag." Dean shot him a pitying look, shook his head, and followed his fiancée to the break room to give everyone their lunch.

Sighing, Jesse took a swig of his soda and wondered how long avoiding his attraction to Lola was going to work. Not that it was working very well right now.

That was close.

Lola took a deep drag from the straw, welcoming the icy cold rush of Sprite in her mouth. Anything to cool herself down. She needed to knock this off. Getting hot and bothered over a man who worked on the same show she did was foolish. Worse was that he was as bad as every other man she knew, and he assumed she was a brainless bimbo who knew more about hair products than being a producer. She did not have the time or energy to fight against that. She had a job to do and she needed to focus on it.

Grabbing her chicken sandwich, she plopped down at the cracked Formica table that filled the middle of the break room. The sharp scent of motor oil and new tires mixed with all the other chemicals that made up the distinct odor of a garage. It was a smell she knew well from her childhood. With a NASCAR driver for an uncle, she'd spent plenty of time around cars.

The burble of conversation flowed around her while she ate. She knew the moment Jesse walked into the room, and that annoyed her. This attraction to him was inconvenient.

Too late, she realized the only free chair was right next to her. Jesse slid into the seat beside her, his shoulder and thigh brushing against hers. Desire shimmered within her, pooling in her belly.

"Sorry," he grunted, inching his chair away. It didn't help much. The table was packed, and she could feel the body heat coming off him in waves that enveloped her.

"No problem." She swallowed a bite of her sandwich and tried not to choke on it.

God. Her hormones rioted, reminding her it had been a while since she'd had some play. She'd been off the market for a while because she'd found depending on a man was emotional suicide, and she wasn't that much of a masochist. There'd been too many guys who never saw anything but her looks, never digging any deeper. Sadly, men seemed to fall into two categories—those who wanted to bone her, and those who wanted to own her. Those in the second category usually fell into the first as well. Her last boyfriend had managed to fool her into believing he wanted a healthy relationship, but instead he'd wanted to control her, make her his pretty, brainless arm-candy. Jackass.

Jesse was no different than all the rest, she reminded herself. She knew the signs by now, and this guy fell into category number one. All he saw, all he wanted, was sex.

But, damn, at the moment, so did she.

She squeezed her thighs together and ignored the ache between them. Every time Jesse moved to drink his soda or eat his burger and fries, his sleeve brushed over her arm and sent goose bumps chasing over her skin. She'd never been so intensely aware of a man in her life.

Reaching past her to grab a packet of ketchup from a pile Andi had dumped in the middle of the table, Jesse shot her a quick grin as his arm slid against the side of her breast. "Sorry."

"It's fine." She wiped any expression off her face, but her nipples tightened instantly and she hunched her shoulders to hide them. Fire shuddered through her, spreading to every inch of her body. So hot, so ready. It was insane how easily he got to her. A quick touch and she lit up like a Christmas tree.

She forced herself to eat, finishing her lunch mechanically. *Just get this over with and get back to work.* That was what she was here for.

Producing a show, and doing it well. One by one, the guys finished their food and began to filter out of the room.

Rising, she gathered the wrappings for her lunch and took them over to the garbage can. Jesse followed her, dumping his own trash in the bin. He turned his head toward her just a bit and pitched his voice low enough so only she could hear. "Hang on a minute before you go."

"Sure." Curiosity zinged through her, but she waited until everyone cleared out, since Jesse obviously didn't want them to listen to what he had to say.

"Thanks." When they were alone, he scrubbed a hand through his short hair, but didn't speak.

God, he was gorgeous, all dark blond hair and bright green eyes. Tall and muscular, with the face of an archangel. Clearing her throat, she arched her eyebrows at him. "What's up, Kasen?"

His eyes met hers, rueful resignation shining in their depths. "It's not working, you know. Pretending this thing between us isn't there."

Sighing, she glanced away for a moment. She wasn't going to be childish and deny the truth of what he was saying. They both knew the score. "There's not really a better option. I value my job, and hooking up with someone on one of my shows will undermine my ability to do my work."

A bit of surprise flashed across his face, as if he was shocked she might take pride in her work, but he nodded. "I understand. I'm not a fan of being the subject of gossip, or of accusations of unprofessionalism."

"So we keep ignoring this...thing." Attraction, desire, boiling hot lust.

"What if no one ever knew about it?"

"Reno's not that big a city, and I don't rely on good luck to keep someone from seeing you leaving my place or me leaving yours." A cheap motel would look even sleazier, but she didn't say that out loud. Best that he not know how often she'd thought through and discarded ideas for how to get away with knocking boots with him.

His broad shoulder dipped in a shrug. "I'm not suggesting we stay in Reno. It's Friday and we're finishing this job early, so we'll all be off until Monday morning. I was planning to go to my dad's cabin on Lake Tahoe. It's a nice spot, and a half hour drive to the nearest town. Come with me."

She opened her mouth, and closed it. Here it was, the perfect excuse and venue to burn off this crazy hankering she had for Jesse Kasen. No one could be as good as she'd built him up to be in her head. Once she found out what the real thing was like, she could finally put it behind her and move on.

There were a million reasons not to—she'd run them through her mind so often she had them memorized. It could hurt the show and make working together afterward uncomfortable. If he was really good in bed, she might want more, and she wouldn't be allowed to have it. If he was really bad in bed... Well...awkward would take on a whole new meaning for her.

It was insane. It was the stupidest thing she could do under the circumstances. But she *had* to know what it was really like. Just this once.

"Okay. This weekend only."

"This weekend only. Out of our systems and over with. I'm on board with that." His gaze dropped to her lips, and he leaned into her space. He moved slowly, giving her plenty of time to back away.

She didn't. Her heart fluttered like a hummingbird, her breathing picking up speed. She was going to do this. She was really going to do this. "Good. We're on the same page."

His breath brushed her skin, but he didn't kiss her. It was a disappointment and a relief that he respected her need to keep work and play separate. She hadn't expected that level of sensitivity from a man who didn't take anything he did with women seriously. Andi had given her that little piece of advice when Lola had first started producing *Revved Up*. Andi had said Jesse was a no-strings-attached kind of guy. Lola was counting on it, considering she could only commit to a weekend.

His eyes pinned her in place, they were so intense. "Yep. I'll get you the directions before we leave today. I'm going straight there after I head home to pack, so show up whenever you're ready." A small smile tucked a dimple into his cheek. "I'm looking forward to it."

So was she. Oh, God, so was she.

Chapter 2

The sun was just sinking behind the Sierra Nevada mountains when Lola pulled up to the cabin. It was a small log building with a long porch that appeared to run all the way around it. Light filtered through the pine trees and sparkled on the lake behind the house. She thought she could see a small dock jutting out into the water, but the cabin blocked her view.

And Jesse's car was parked in front, so she was in the right place.

Nerves twisted in her belly. She drew in a slow, calming breath and resisted the urge to spin her Mustang around and peel out down the dirt driveway. But then the door to the cabin opened and Jesse stepped out. He wasn't wearing a shirt, and the view was pretty spectacular. Broad shoulders sloped down into heavy pecs sprinkled with hair, and hard ridges of abs tapered to a narrow waist. She wanted to slide her hands over his naked skin, wanted to know if the curls on his chest would be crisp or soft under her palms. Warmth pulsed through her body, settling in to ache between her thighs.

She wanted him. She always wanted him.

He propped his long, muscular form against one of the porch posts, his gaze meeting hers through the windshield. There was a challenge in his expression. Daring her to go through with this.

Too bad she'd never been one to back down from a challenge.

Easing up on the brake, she steered her Mustang in to park next to his classic Porsche Spyder. The car was almost as pretty to look at as the man. Almost. She grinned, slipped her key from the ignition, and gathered her purse and overnight bag from the passenger seat. Then she squared her shoulders and climbed out.

Jesse made no move toward her. His gaze slid over her while he waited for her to come to him. He did nothing to rush her, just let her decide when she was ready. But a slow smile curled his lips, flashing straight white teeth. The sight set her heart to fluttering, which made her roll her eyes at herself and move toward the house. Time to put up or shut up. Or put out, as the case may be.

"I'll take that," he said as she mounted the porch steps, reaching for her small duffel.

She handed it over, electricity sparking through her as their fingers brushed. When he turned for the door, she caught his arm, pulling him around to face her. "Wait. I need to..."

Rising up on tiptoe, she brushed her lips across his. It was their first kiss. And she'd already agreed to sleep with him. Clearly, she was insane. That knowledge didn't even make her pause. She swept her tongue along the seam of his lips, dipping in to taste him. She curled her fingers around his shoulders, testing the resilience of flesh and muscle there. Heat over steel. His fingers came up to bracket her jaw, drawing her closer as he thrust his tongue into her mouth. The breath tangled in her chest and her heart thumped against her ribs. His hot, masculine flavor filled her mouth, and she moaned. Excitement exploded deep inside her as their tongues twined together. More. That was the only thought that crossed her mind. *More.*

She arched toward him, trying to tell him what she needed without breaking the kiss. Suckling his bottom lip, she bit down on the soft flesh. A groan reverberated through his chest. He snaked an arm around her waist, hauling her flush against him. It was the first time they'd ever had full-body contact, and it left her breathless. Desire washed over her, her sex contracting on emptiness. The intensity of it shocked her. She dug her nails into his shoulders, not sure if she wanted to push him away or pull him closer.

It didn't matter, in the end. He slanted his mouth over hers, twining his tongue with hers. The heady flavor of him burst over her taste buds again—coffee, hot male, and something that was uniquely Jesse. He spun her around, leaving her dizzy and clinging to him. The creak of the door's hinges and the thump of her bag hitting the floor told her he'd backed her into the house.

He pressed her up against the wall beside the door, every delicious muscle rubbing against her softer curves. Dipping forward, he slid his tongue down the side of her neck and nipped at the sensitive tendon at the base of her throat. She moaned and let her head fall back against the smooth wooden wall.

"Jesse..."

"Yeah?" His palms skimmed down her sides to curve over her hips.

A breathy laugh escaped her. "Shouldn't we...I don't know, have dinner or something? Not just get straight to sex?"

He paused for a moment. "Why?"

She had no clue, not one good reason why they shouldn't go at it like rabbits. Her hormones did a happy little tap dance at the thought. "Never mind."

"I made lasagna. It won't be done baking for another forty-five minutes." He scraped the edge of his teeth against her neck. "Let's use the time wisely."

She chuckled. Now that he mentioned it, she could smell dinner cooking. The aroma of spices in the marinara sauce curled into her nostrils. The scent just hadn't registered while he'd been kissing her. Nothing except him had impinged on her consciousness. "Okay."

"Okay. Great." Then he pressed his lips to hers again, and the rest of the world melted away. He settled his weight on her, holding her to the wall. Her breasts flattened against his chest, and her nipples became aching peaks under the pressure. She wanted his mouth there. The idea alone made her whimper. She threaded her fingers through his hair, savored the rough silk of it.

The hard ridge of his shaft pressed into the juncture of her thighs. She tried to part them for him, wanting him where he could do the most to ease her need, but her skirt hampered her. Waves of lust crashed over her and she arched into him. Her body throbbed, her sex fisting on nothingness. She wanted to be filled. His palm curled over her breast, thumbing the tip.

It was too much, a lightning strike of sensation from her breast to her core. A harsh sound broke from her throat, and she tried to climb him. She needed him inside her. Right now. She sucked in a ragged breath, her nails clawing into his shoulders. "Jesse!"

"Damn, Lola." He wrestled her skirt up and her panties down while she tugged at the button on his jeans, jerking open the zipper. He fished into his pocket and came out with a shiny foil packet before he shoved his pants off and kicked them aside.

"Hurry," she gasped. It was the only thought she had left. Hurry. *Now.*

He sheathed himself in the condom with quick efficiency and lifted her against the wall. She wrapped her legs tightly around his waist, and then finally, *finally* she felt the blunt probing of his erection at her slick opening. She squeezed her legs around his flanks, urging him onward. His fingers dug into her buttocks painfully, but it only sharpened her pleasure. Easing his grip, he let her sink down on him.

The stretch was exquisite, reminding her just how long it had been since she'd had sex. Too long. Tingles raced over her skin and she shivered at the hot ecstasy streaking through her. When he withdrew, she moaned. The amazing glide made her body clench in reaction. *More.* She wanted more. Needed it.

Arching his hips, he slammed back inside her, seating himself to the hilt. Shock robbed her of breath, and she raked her nails down his back. He hissed, the muscles in his shoulders jerking. But he didn't stop what he was doing. He pistoned in and out of her, riding her hard against the wall, and she moved with him. The way he filled her to the limit each time made her gasp, but she loved it. Pressing her hips forward, she tried to take him deeper. Her thighs protested the sudden workout but she ignored the discomfort. Her entire world had narrowed down to the need to come. Only orgasm mattered.

The breath rushed in pants from her lungs and sweat slipped down her skin. He buried his face in the crook of her neck and his stubble abraded her flesh. Every sensation shoved her closer to the edge of climax. He sank inside her, rotating his pelvis against her sex. A whimper broke from her and gooseflesh skittered down her limbs. She tightened her inner muscles around his shaft in revenge and he groaned, the sound ragged with desperation.

He turned his head and bit the side of her throat. Stars burst behind her eyelids as she came in one explosive rush of ecstasy. "Jesse!"

His hands jerked her thighs wider apart, and he rode her harder, driving toward his own orgasm. She cried out as he slid deeper than he had before and ground himself against her. A great shudder passed through him and he groaned long and loud as he came.

Silence fell over the room, broken only by their panting breath. Her muscles relaxed and she slumped against him, her cheek resting on his broad shoulder.

"You had a condom in your pocket." Her voice emerged soft, bemused.

He hummed a little. "I put it there when I saw you drive up. I bought a new box for the weekend."

"A whole box, huh?"

"I'm an optimist."

A breathy chuckle escaped her, and she patted his shoulder. "I appreciate that about you, sugar."

"I aim to please." He dropped his forehead to hers, his teeth flashing in a smile.

She grinned back. "Your aim is excellent."

He laughed outright at that, stepping back to let her feet slide to the floor. He tugged away what remained of their clothing, dropping it to the floor. Then he scooped her into his arms and carried her to the big leather sofa to lay her down.

"I need to clean up. One second." He walked away and, a few minutes later, she heard the toilet flush.

When he came back, he sat down beside her and tugged her into his lap, maneuvering them until he stretched out on his back and she sprawled across his chest. It shouldn't have been a comfortable position, but it was. A sigh eased out of her, and she closed her eyes, letting the postcoital bliss wash over her. She drifted in that haze of pleasure for endless moments while he stroked light circles over her back.

Beeping sounded from the kitchen, making them both jolt a bit.

"That's dinner. I'll be right back."

Jesse dropped a quick kiss on the top of her head, set her on the couch and rolled easily to his feet. She enjoyed the view of his naked backside retreating, and she also got an unobstructed look at the tattoo that started at the base of his skull, spread down his shoulders and covered most of his back. She'd had no idea it was so large. With the shirts he wore at work, she'd only ever seen the very top of it. It looked like Japanese art she'd seen in pictures. There was a huge red dragon at the top, surrounded by swirling black marks that she thought might symbolize clouds. The scales of the dragon somehow merged with the orange scales of an intricately detailed koi fish that swam through water at the base of his spine, and lotus blossoms floated on the water. It was beautiful. She'd never been one for tattoos, but she liked his.

She wanted to lick her way from one end of it to the other.

Chapter 3

Jesus, it had been incredible. Worth the buildup. Jesse's body still buzzed with the aftermath, better than any drug. He grinned, pulling the lasagna out of the oven to let it cool. He uncorked a bottle of red wine and poured a couple of glasses. Nothing like some good booze to add to the high of good sex.

Dishing out a green salad onto two plates, he made sure to leave room for the main course. He called over his shoulder. "How hungry are you?"

Her voice came from right behind him. "That's not a frozen Stouffer's meal."

Glancing back, he lifted an eyebrow. "I said I *made* lasagna. It's not that hard. It just takes a little time, which I had to kill while I was waiting for you."

"That's a lot of Italian food. You must have been really confident I'd show." She propped her hands on her hips, which made her bare breasts bounce. "What if I hadn't?"

"Then I'd have had leftovers to last the whole weekend, wouldn't I?" He brushed his lips over hers, and he was rewarded when she fitted her lush body to his, deepening the kiss. Filling one palm with her breast, he tweaked the tip before he stepped back with a smile. "But I had hope that you'd decide to take me up on my invitation. And here you are."

"Here I am." She spread her arms, sweeping them down to motion to herself. "Here, and ready to eat."

"All right, then." He used a spatula to give them both a good-size portion. "Grab the wine and the forks, I've got the plates."

"Silverware drawer is...?"

"To the right of the fridge."

She got the utensils out and followed him to the living room. He set the food on the coffee table and settled on the sofa. His stomach rumbled, reminding him of what he'd just done to work up an appetite. And what he had plans to do in order to work up an even bigger craving for breakfast.

"This is delicious." Lola dug into her food with gusto. "I can't believe you cooked this from scratch."

He took a bite of his dinner. Yeah, it had come out just right. Cheesy, meaty, just enough spice to give the marinara some tang. "Don't get too excited. This is one of the few dishes I know how to make. This, waffles, and chicken noodle soup."

"That's a pretty random combination." Her gaze danced with amusement as she sipped her wine.

Shrugging, he forked a cherry tomato from the salad into his mouth. "My dad was an amateur chef. He used to win the chili cook-off at some of the local festivals every year."

"Chef and mechanic." Her eyes crinkled at the corners. "Your mother was a lucky lady."

"Yeah." Too bad she hadn't thought so. Jesse's good mood dampened a bit, but he pushed aside that old bitterness. His father had been dead for years, and his mother had left long before that. It was all long over. Done.

Lola tilted her head, glancing at him while she ate, as if she wasn't sure what to make of his sudden terseness. When she didn't question him about it, he breathed a sigh of relief. They fell into a companionable silence while they finished their dinners.

She set aside her plate, picking up her wine to drink. "So, tell me about you."

"We're getting personal, are we?" He flashed a sinful grin, letting his gaze slide over her naked body. Having her curled up beside him nude had been almost too much to resist during dinner, but he had her all weekend. He had some time to relish the slow burn of anticipation. "Wouldn't it be easier if we just stuck to the sex?"

"I don't know. I've never done just sex before. And maybe I like to know what I'm dealing with." Her shoulder dipped in a shrug. "Start with something easy. Tell me about your tattoo."

He grabbed the back of the couch for leverage, leaned forward a little, and twisted to let her look at it. "I got it in Japan. I studied there for a year in high school."

"Oh, yeah?" She ran her finger along one of the shapes on his back, he thought the top of the koi. "You got that while you were in high school?"

"I was eighteen." Barely old enough to know his head from his ass, but he'd never regretted getting the tattoo.

"Eighteen? Wouldn't that have been your senior year? You didn't miss having your senior year with your friends?"

"No." He snorted. "I was happy to go, and my parents were happy to send me." Tension flooded his muscles when he could all but feel her curiosity pique. Yep, getting personal was a bad idea. His hand fisted on the leather sofa, and he forced his fingers to loosen.

Her nails tapped against his spine. "Why?"

Sighing, he made himself answer. This was old news. It was just...being around a woman like Lola was stirring everything up. His usual type tended more toward one-nighters with barflies—women who wore their hair too big and their clothes too tight. Nothing like his mother. Or Lola.

"That was the year my parents split up for good. It had been building for a long time—Mom left and came back, left and came back." And Jesse was pretty sure his dad had spent the rest of his life waiting for her to come back again. "But things had gotten a lot worse, and I was just as glad not to stick around and watch the end. I got the tattoo when I found out my mother had filed for divorce." He cleared his throat. Old news or not, he wished they were talking about something else. *Anything* else but this. "This tat style is called Irezumi. It's done by hand, and you have to find a master who'll do it. Only they make themselves hard to find because tattooing in Japan used to be a way to mark criminals, so it's still a little taboo."

She hesitated, as if she wanted to protest the topic change, but she didn't. Her fingertip drew a curved line up his back until she reached the top of the tattoo at his neck. Goose bumps broke out on his flesh at her touch and his shaft twitched in reaction to her nearness. She toyed with the hair at his nape. "I didn't even know there were different schools of thought about tattoos, other than those who like them and those who don't."

"I take it you're in the 'those who don't' category." He resettled into his seat, untwisting from the slightly awkward position.

She rocked her hand back and forth through the air. "I don't dislike them, but I don't want one. My sister has a couple, and my uncle has a big one on his arm. Everyone seems to have them now. I think I'm one of the few holdouts left in the world."

"My dad didn't have one, but Uncle Gary does. Dean has one too, on his leg."

She hesitated again. "I've never really heard you talk about any family but your cousin and his parents. Do you see your mom often?"

"Not since she bailed. She got in touch after she started seeing me on TV, but it wasn't any kind of genuine interest in reuniting, just a money thing. Mom's always been high maintenance, liked the finer things in life and having people admire her." Like Lola, in her fancy clothes and using her pretty face and body to get what she wanted. His mother had the same beauty and tactics. "She traded up after she left my dad."

Her face flooded with sympathy he didn't want. A lot of people had it worse than he did, and his life was just fine, thanks. But her gaze had gone soft with compassion. "That's really sad."

"It is what it is." He pushed to his feet, grabbing their empty plates. "Enjoy the rest of your wine while I clean up."

Conversation over. Probably not the best way to get laid again, running away from the woman he wanted to shag, but he wasn't a fan of digging into the past. It was, by definition, over. He didn't dwell on it. It wasn't that he had a problem talking to Lola about *himself*. If she wanted to know something, it was fine. But they didn't need to bring up his parents. His parents weren't him and he wasn't them. He tried not to think about his mom very often, and that had proven impossible with Lola around for comparison.

He took the dishes to the kitchen, washed them, stored the leftovers, and wiped down the counters so the crumbs wouldn't attract any of the insects and other pests that lived in the woods. He'd learned that lesson the hard way the first time he'd come here without his dad.

Lola's glass clinked against the counter as she set it down. "Listen, Jesse... I didn't mean to press on a sore point. I was just curious and I wanted..." She sighed. "It doesn't matter what I wanted. I'm sorry."

She'd put her clothes back on. Her shirt was haphazardly buttoned, but she was dressed. A shame, that.

"I prefer to focus on the here and now." He blew out a breath, turning to settle back against the sink. "I can change the now. Can't do anything about the past."

Her brows furrowed and she shook her head. "The past defines us and makes us who we are."

"I try not to let it define me. I like to think I can always change, and I'm not stuck with whatever the past dished out to me." He ran a finger along the neckline of her shirt, down to where it met the curve of her cleavage. Her breath caught, her nipples jutting against the fabric. He grinned. "Besides, the here and now seems pretty good to me."

She licked her lower lip, leaning into his touch. "I can't argue with you there."

"Well, then." He bent forward and kissed her collarbone, savoring her sweet scent and the heat that began to pour through his body. "Since we agree on that, what would you like to do with our now?"

A chuckle bubbled out of her. "It's not very sexy, but...I'd really like to use a bathroom. And then have you give me a tour of the bedroom."

He snorted, nipping her earlobe with his teeth before he stepped back. "That can be arranged. Bathroom is the first door off the hallway, bedroom's at the end of the hall. I'll get your bag and meet you on the mattress."

That made her laugh that smoky laugh of hers. She rose on tiptoe and popped a kiss on his mouth. "Thanks, sugar."

Sugar. That was the second time she'd called him that. He wasn't accustomed to pet names from women, and he'd never have figured Lola as the kind to use them. It was odd, but not bad.

He wandered into the living room and scooped up her duffel and his discarded clothes, locking the front door—something they'd overlooked earlier. At least they'd made it inside before they'd gotten as busy as a pair of rabbits. Then again, the nearest neighbors were a couple of miles away, so they weren't likely to be caught. There was a fun possibility to consider.

He could hear the water running in the sink as he walked by the bathroom door. Dropping her bag with his on the floor by the bed, he tossed his clothes into the hamper.

"Well, I feel better." Lola came into the room, finger-combing her long hair.

"Glad to hear it." He grinned at her. "So, what position would you like to try next?"

The question seemed to catch her off-guard, and he couldn't keep a naughty smile off his face as her cheeks went rosy pink. He didn't think he'd ever seen her blush before.

"I'd like to be on top." She was quick to rally and arched one eyebrow regally. "How long can you hold your breath, Kasen? I'm going to ride your face."

The blunt response surprised and pleased him. He laughed. "I don't know if I can set any kind of record for holding my breath, but I'll give it my all if that's what you want. Whatever turns you on."

Frowning, she bit her lower lip. "Huh."

"What?" He sat down on the bed, pulling one leg up onto the mattress.

A little half-smile twisted her mouth. "I've never had a guy focus on what turns *me* on. Don't get me wrong, I had fun and so did they, but I've always known part of what got them off was having someone who looked like me in their bed. I was a conquest for them."

Her candor was refreshing. He liked that she didn't dance around the topic, which was one thing that made her nothing like his mom. "Sounds like a bunch of jerks."

"In the end, yeah. They did leave me wanting, in more ways than one." She tilted her head, her eyes crinkling. "I like to tell my sister that guys want to own me or bone me. Or both."

"Jerks," he repeated. Though didn't he fit neatly into one of those categories? He fought a wince. At least he didn't fall into both. He'd never wanted to own a woman in his life. Most of the time, he was fine with seeing them go after a bit of fun. He did feel the need to justify himself a little, which almost never happened. "You're not a conquest to me. I like the way you look, but if there wasn't a whole lot of chemistry between us, it wouldn't matter if you were the most gorgeous woman alive."

Though she just might be. He'd never seen a woman more beautiful than her. But he hadn't lied. He wouldn't be diving into bed with a coworker just because she was pretty. It was because the sparks were too hot to resist. Which still didn't make it a smart move, but it would be over and done in a couple days.

"That's good to know." She bent to retrieve a brush from her bag and ran it through her satiny hair.

He propped himself against the headboard, watching her for a minute before he spoke again. "Do you want me on my back now, or do you have something else in mind first?"

Just seeing the sinful grin that bloomed on her face got him hot. His erection stiffened and he decided to put on a show for her, since they were focusing on what turned her on. Sliding his hand down his belly, he let his fingers stroke over the length of his shaft. When she glanced at him, saw how he touched himself, she drew in a quick breath. Her hand clenched around the brush handle. "Oh, my."

He grinned, rolling his thumb over the head of his erection. "See something you like?"

Her gaze darkened as it locked on what he was doing. "Y'all know how to make an impression, sugar."

"Your accent gets thicker when you're turned on." His heart hammered in his ears, his breathing picking up speed. "Take your clothes off."

Yes, he wanted her naked again. Preferably for every single minute of this weekend. He saw no reason for them to leave the bed. Who needed food anyway? Sex was much more important. Especially sex with Lola.

Tossing aside the brush, she slipped the first few buttons free on her top, then tugged it over her head and dropped it on top of her bag. Her shoes and skirt came next, and then her bra. He groaned as her breasts were freed and he saw how taut the tips were. Just right for sucking. She wriggled her hips a little as she pushed down her panties, and he licked his lips as the soft thatch of curls between her thighs came into view. "Come here."

"Not yet." Her voice was a breathless rush. "Don't stop playing with yourself. I want to watch. I want to play with you too."

He palmed his erection for her, stroking the length of it. "Is this what you want?"

Now it was her turn to lick her lips, and she nodded. She sat beside him on the bed, sliding her fingertips up the inside of his thigh. His muscles clenched at the sensation, anticipating where she was going to touch him next.

"So many fun places I could start." The grin that lit her face was as mischievous as it was naughty. She cupped the soft sac between his legs, fondling him gently.

Jesus. He had to take his hand off his shaft or he was going to come before he got inside her. And he wanted inside her, wanted that tight sheath squeezing around him.

Dancing her fingers upward, she bypassed his erection to circle his navel, then drifted upward to tease his nipples. The discs tightened and he choked on a breath.

"Nice." Humming, she leaned forward to flick her tongue across one flat nipple, grazing it with her teeth.

"Yes, lick me. Anywhere you want." He knew exactly where he wanted that talented mouth of hers.

Chuckling, she straightened and ran her fingertips up to caress his throat and jaw, then tickled the end of his nose. He snorted and turned his face away. "Brat."

"Maybe a little." She zoomed one fingernail down his body and slid it straight up his shaft. The sensation was tickling and pleasurable and *intense*. He shuddered, forcing himself to relax and not to pounce on her. She wanted to play, so he let her, but he wasn't sure he'd ever been this hard before in his life. Bending forward, she blew a cool stream of air over his overheated flesh, making his erection jerk in response. He closed his eyes, not sure how much more he could take.

His entire body jolted when he felt her tongue slide around the head of his shaft. Then she took him deep into her mouth. His hips arched off the bed, and his fingers tangled in her hair. "Lola!"

A hum quivered along his shaft and he hissed out a breath, heat punching through him. The sight of her sucking him was the most erotic thing he'd ever laid eyes on. She worked him with her mouth and hand, pumping him until groans ripped from his throat. She just sucked him harder.

His lungs bellowed, and he fisted his hands in the sheets. The sensual torment just might kill him. "Jesus. *Christ.*"

She pulled back, leaving him shuddering and damn near ready to beg her to finish. Her eyebrow arched. "I want you on your back now."

"Sadist," he grumbled, but he slid down until he was flat against the mattress. "You going to clock me on holding my breath?"

"Nope." Gingerly, she swung her leg over his head, settling on her knees over his face. "Are you sure you're okay with this, sugar?"

"Come here." He grabbed her hips and pulled her downward. He felt her waver as she tried to maintain her balance, and he assumed she held onto the headboard. His attention was more focused on sliding his tongue from one end of her slit to the other. Her juices coated his tongue, and he groaned against her flesh. God, he loved the taste of her. She whimpered and began to move against him, riding his face as she'd promised. He kissed, suckled, and licked her, driving her toward orgasm as quickly as he could. He felt her thighs begin to quake and her moans kissed his ears. Yeah, she was close. So, he curled his tongue around her swollen little nub before sucking it hard. Crying out, she ground herself down on his mouth and chin as she climaxed.

"Jesse!" Pushing away from the headboard, she moved down to give him a kiss hot enough to scorch. His erection gave a jerk that reminded him only one of them had gotten to come. The intensity built, sharpening to a cutting edge that had him hanging on to his self-restraint by a mere thread. Holding his face between her palms, she said, "We need a condom. Right now."

"Top drawer." He tipped his chin toward the nightstand.

She purred, "How convenient."

It took her under a minute to slide the rubber over his erection. Thank God. He seized her hips, jerking her into place over him. "Ride me."

She sank down on him in one swift motion, and they both moaned. He set his hands at her waist, pulling her tight to the base of his shaft while he shoved upward. The rhythm she set for them was fast and wild, and she rolled her hips to increase the friction. Her breathing came in little gasps that only turned him on more. He buried himself inside her, and she was slick and taut around him. So good. So damn good. Reaching between them, he pressed his fingertip directly on her nub and she cried out. The way her inner muscles spasmed around his shaft made lava flow through his veins. Her movements grew more frantic, and he knew she was close.

He watched her brown eyes lose focus as she concentrated on coming. He gritted his teeth to fight his own orgasm as her hot, wet sex contracted on his shaft. Her sexy little whimpers almost killed him as her climax went on. He wasn't ready for this to be over quite yet, so he forced himself to think about anything other than what they were doing. Rebuilding a carburetor, replacing spark plugs, fixing the timing belt on his Spyder.

When he felt reasonably sure he wasn't going to go off like a teenager in the backseat of his parents' car, he began to grind himself subtly upward. The way she gasped told him she noticed his hard-on hadn't gone anywhere. Her hands braced against his chest, and she moved with him, slowly at first, building in tempo until they'd gone wild again. He bracketed her waist with his hands, holding her aloft while he powered into her hard and fast, their skin smacking together, the bed creaking beneath them. Fire licked at his flesh, the need to come driving him onward. He pulled her down hard, rotating his pelvis against her sex, knowing he wouldn't last much longer, and he wanted to take her with him.

A desperate little wail broke from her lips as she shuddered over him. "I'm coming, Jesse. Oh, my *God*. I'm coming again. Jesse, Jesse, Jesse!"

He loved his name on her lips, and the exquisite feel of her clenching around his shaft was more than enough to make him explode inside her. A rush of sensation and need gripped his gut, dragging everything out of him until there was nothing left. But he couldn't help the smile that curved his lips.

Definitely worth the last few months of buildup. Hell, yes. This weekend was the best idea he'd ever had.

Chapter 4

Lola's body ached pleasantly, the way it could only after several rounds of energetic sex. She couldn't help but grin as she grabbed a wrench and went to work under the hood of Jesse's car. He'd still been passed out in bed when she woke up, wired and unable to fall back asleep. So, she was doing something productive with her Saturday morning. Every now and then, she liked to get her hands dirty.

She just felt *good* today. A nice buzz tingled along her nerves, and she was definitely riding the high from the night before. When Jesse woke up, she'd ride him too, and keep the buzz going. It was the best plan she'd had in a long time.

The small car repair wouldn't take her much longer. Her uncle would be proud she hadn't forgotten everything he'd taught her.

"What *the hell* are you doing?" Jesse's voice was an incredulous, angry growl right behind her.

Lola jolted, but managed not to hit her head on the underside of the raised hood. Oh, damn. Caught red-handed. Or greasy-handed. She winced, her high fading a little. Nothing to do but bravado her way out of this one. She pasted a smile on her face, grabbed a rag to wipe her fingers off on, and straightened to face him. "Fixing your timing belt. I could hear your Spyder whining all the way down the road when you left the garage."

A muscle in his jaw ticked. "I was going to take care of that. Myself."

"But you were distracted by getting ready for the weekend with me, I know. Lasagna, condoms." She widened her grin. "Now you don't have to worry about the car."

His eyes narrowed to slits. "Unless you did something that completely destroyed my priceless classic car."

Now, that was going a little far. Her brows contracted. "It's a phenomenal car, but it's hardly *priceless*."

"It is if my father and I restored it from a bucket of rust together. *Right before he died.*"

Oh. Her smile fell away and her belly knotted. "I'm sorry, Jesse. I swear I didn't mess up your Spyder at all. You can check."

Grunting, he came forward to do just that, brushing against her as he moved. He got his hands in the engine, inspecting the belt and tensioner.

She hovered, worried now that she had somehow made a mistake. She started babbling even though she knew now was probably a good time to shut up. "Look, I didn't know you could cook, right? Is it really so impossible that I might know something about cars? I was interested in producing *Revved Up* for a reason. I could have gone after another show if I wanted to, but I asked for this one. I know my way around cars, I really do."

"Okay. It looks like you did this right." He took a breath, rolled his shoulders, visibly forcing himself to relax. Glancing back at her, the corners of his eyes crinkled. "Maybe just tell me next time instead of diving under the hood of my ride. I'm a mechanic, so I'm pretty territorial where my cars are concerned. Especially this car."

"Noted." Her nose wrinkled. "I've been wanting to look under your hood for a while. I couldn't resist, and I wasn't thinking. But I wouldn't want you messing with my Mustang without asking. Sorry about that, sugar."

A little grin eased the tension out of his face. "You've been wanting to get under my hood, huh?"

"Shut up, pervert." She huffed out a laugh.

One of his blond brows cocked and his grin turned lecherous. "I didn't hear you complaining last night."

No woman in her right mind would have complained about last night. And there was Jesse with nothing but a pair of faded jeans clinging to his muscular thighs. Mm-hm.

He nodded to the engine. "So, why don't we finish this together?"

"I thought you'd never ask, sugar." The smile she gave him made his gaze darken with lust, just as she'd intended. Bending over beside him, she held in a sigh when their arms rubbed together and warmth heated her belly.

"Where'd you learn to do this?" His hands soon turned as blackened as hers as they set the belt on the right course, checking the crank, cam, and sprockets for timing marks.

"My uncle." She grabbed the wrench she had balanced on the engine block and used it on the crankshaft to move the belt around a few revolutions while Jesse made sure the belt stayed on course.

"So, when do I get to get under *your* hood?" He glanced over at her fourteen-year-old fire-engine-red Mustang. It was a beauty, but definitely not one of the vintage cars he was used to working on. She doubted he was as keen to play with her car as she had been to play with his.

"I should probably get something newer, but my parents bought it just before they passed away." She shrugged, grabbing the timing cover so they could reaffix it. "I haven't been able to talk myself into getting rid of it, even though it's at that weird stage where it's not new, but not yet a classic. It's just old."

"Those awkward teen years." He nodded sagely, and she chuckled. "Don't worry, they age out of that phase and turn into classics. No reason why you should get rid of it if it's running well."

She made an incredulous noise. "I keep my baby purring like a kitten."

He helped her put the cover back on. "I'll refrain from making a dirty joke, since you already called me a pervert."

That cracked her up, and he laughed with her. She bumped his shoulder with hers. "Come on, let's finish."

"Whatever you want, honey." They reconnected the battery, and then Jesse went around to turn over the engine. The car started immediately and didn't give the irritating whine that had made her want to fix it in the first place.

She leaned to the side, waving a hand at him to shut the engine down. "Looks good!"

Climbing out of the car, he came to join her while she tossed the wrench into her toolbox. The expanse of his naked chest was right in front of her, and it was all she could do not to lick one of his nipples. Maybe bite it a little while she was at it. A flush raced up her cheeks, and she was pretty sure her expression gave away what she was thinking. Not that she was trying to hide it.

He ran a thumb across her cheek. "You've got grease on you. Time for a shower."

"Okay."

Bending forward to grab her toolbox, he walked over to stuff it in her trunk. "Let me put that away for you, so you don't get any more ideas about touching my Spyder without me here to supervise."

"I won't!" She had to admire the fact that he hadn't freaked out on her. Most men she knew would have read her the riot act for dreaming of touching their cars. She would have reamed anyone who'd done what she did. *Way to go, Lola.* Seeing a problem and fixing it was her nature. She hadn't been thinking of what Jesse might have wanted, and she'd stepped over the line. He'd called her on it, but he hadn't been a jerk about it. He really was a *nice* man. She didn't know why that startled her so much, but it did.

"What?"

She shook her head, forcing her mind back to why she was here. It wasn't to appreciate Jesse's personality. She let a slow smile form on her lips, running her gaze down his body. "Nothing. I want you. In the shower works just fine for me, sugar."

His features tightened with lust, his gaze sharpening and his pupils expanding. "Good. Come here."

He had it bad.

If he didn't, he'd have blown a gasket over her laying a finger on his car. He loved that car. Working on it with her had been interesting, something he'd never done with a woman before. Only he and his dad had ever touched the Spyder in the years he'd owned it. True, the repair today had been pretty simple, but she definitely knew more about the inside of an engine than the average customer at the garage. Which was surprising, in a really good way.

She led the way into the house and a warm sense of what might have been contentment wrapped around him. It was foolish to enjoy this so much. His time with her was ticking down to an inevitable end. He'd told himself to dive into this and experience it to the fullest, but there was such a thing as getting in over his head. He rubbed a hand over the nape of his neck, sighing. He liked having her near, liked the way they sparked off each other and made each other laugh. They had little in common, and it made no sense, but there it was.

This was not a good sign.

His mouth dried as he watched Lola strip on her way to the bathroom. She draped her lacy bra across the back of the couch, giving him a provocative glance over her shoulder. All the blood rushed from his brain to fill his erection, which ached with the need to be buried inside her.

He unfastened his jeans, shoving them down as he followed her. There was no way he could resist. He licked his lips when she wriggled out of her panties and left them in the hallway before she entered the bathroom. Damn, but she had one fine backside. High and round. He groaned as he watched her lean forward to turn on the shower.

"Ready, sugar?" she drawled out, her voice sweet and Southern.

He gestured to his stiffened erection. "What do you think?"

"Excellent." Winking, she stepped under the spray and crooked her finger at him.

He was across the small room in two strides, crowding her into the shower stall to make sure her damp curves rubbed against his body. Hot water sluiced down him and steam filled the room. He bent forward to catch a droplet of moisture that quivered on the tip of her nipple, curling his tongue around the tight peak. She swayed into him, her hands sliding into his hair. Her grip tightened painfully when he bit down on her breast. The sting did nothing to dissuade him.

Slipping her fingers out of his hair, she stroked across his shoulder and down to tweak one of his nipples. Gooseflesh broke over his limbs. God, he loved her hands on him. She tugged on his chest hair before her nail flicked hard over the flat disc. He shuddered, releasing her breast to straighten. She took the opportunity to drop her hands to his shaft, stroking the length of it.

"You know, I should really make it up to you about the car." She sank to her knees before him, flashing the kind of smile that made his heart hammer.

"Oh, yeah. You might need to make it up to me more than once."

She chuckled, taking him into her mouth. He had to grit his teeth to hold on to a modicum of control. He didn't want this to end that quickly. The jets of water that poured over his skin did little to help in that area. It only added to the sensations that crashed into him. Lola took him deep, and he watched her cheeks hollow out as she sucked him. She met his gaze and the look in her eyes told him she knew exactly how she affected him. Damn, but she was perfect. Nothing else mattered right now. This moment, with her, was perfect.

Sweat broke out on his forehead, the salty beads combining with the spray of water pelting his body. Her tongue slid down the underside of his shaft, and then her mouth opened to take in one of his balls. She sucked him hard, her teeth scraping ever so lightly on the sensitive skin.

"Jesus *Christ*." His hands shot out to brace himself on the shower walls. Choking on a harsh moan, he gave a full-body shudder.

She stroked her palm up and down his erection, her rhythm fast enough to shove him right over the edge. Lust boiled through him, and his lungs burned as he tried to drag in enough oxygen. One, two, three more swift strokes of her hand and he lost it. His muscles jerked and he came into the air, groaning out his orgasm.

"Lola!"

She continued to work his shaft with her fingers, her tongue teasing his balls, until he shivered and had to pull away. His heart still pounded in his ears, his lungs heaving for air. He dropped down, kneeling before her. The water rained down on them and he pulled her close, pressing his forehead to hers. "That was definitely the way to start the morning."

A giggle was her answer, and she wrapped her arms around him. "No question. Though do you think we should maybe use the shower for showering?"

"You don't want to test how long the water heater holds out?"

"Not hardly."

"Well, all right." He swatted her backside, then forced his muscles to work enough to haul them both to their feet.

Dipping forward, he kissed her again. He had to. The taste of her was something he'd never get his fill of. Sweet and spicy and totally Lola. He'd get as much of it as he could for as long as he could, because he would be walking away after this weekend was over. A deal was a deal. If something painful twisted through him at the thought, he ignored it.

They washed themselves quickly, since the water heater *was* starting to give out on them. He held open the shower door for her, letting her hop out to grab a towel, and then he did the same.

After she'd dried off, she draped the terry cloth over the towel rack, moved over to the vanity, and bent forward to grab her brush. Jesse couldn't resist. He dipped down and ran the tip of his tongue along the cleft in her rounded buttocks. Her body tightened and he felt a delicate shiver course through her. He knelt down behind her. Slipping his fingers between her thighs, he eased into her. She was soaking wet and it had nothing to do with the recent shower. A soft moan echoed in the room.

He glanced up and met her gaze in the mirror. "What? You didn't think I'd leave you unsatisfied, did you?"

Chapter 5

"Y ou don't have cable or satellite up here, do you?"

Jesse opened one eye to give her an incredulous look. She couldn't be serious. After the last round of sex, his brain wasn't functioning well enough to remember his own name, let alone worry about cable. "Did you see a TV anywhere? My old man came out here to get away from the world. Fishing, tinkering on his car, sitting on the porch with a cold beer. If he wanted television, he went to the bar a few miles down the shore."

She glanced at the old clock on the bedside table, swinging her legs over the side of the bed to stand. "Then we're headed to the bar."

"You have a show you just can't miss? You couldn't set it to record on your DVR or something?" He ran a hand down his face. She *really* had to be kidding. He sat up and tried to catch her arm to haul her back into bed, but she danced out of his reach, laughing.

"I did set it to record, but no, I have to see this live." She dug through her bag until she came up with some clothes. He watched her wiggle and bounce getting her underwear, shirt, and jean skirt on. She arched her eyebrows at him. "You don't have to come along if you don't want to, Kasen. Just give me directions and I'll be back in a couple of hours."

"The hell you say." He rolled out of bed and stuffed himself into some clean clothes, glowering at her. "You're not ditching me to go hang out in a bar. I get the *whole* weekend with you."

"Of course, sugar." She chortled. "Don't get your boxers in a wad. I was just getting you to hurry up. It's already noon. We need to go."

He opened his mouth, closed it again. There was nothing he could say that wasn't going to come out a four-letter word, so he just shook his head, stuck his wallet in his back pocket, and led the way down the hall. The woman was amazing. He'd never met anyone who turned him on or pissed him off quite so fast. When it came to her, he reacted.

He wasn't sure if he liked that or not. It probably depended on which end of the turned on–pissed off spectrum he was at.

"Hey, where are we going?" she called when he turned for the back door. "The cars are the other way."

"I said the bar was a few miles down the *shore*." He grinned over his shoulder at her, opening the door to point toward the boat tethered at the end of the dock. "This is the fastest way to make sure you don't miss your soap opera."

"It's Saturday, smart-ass. Soaps are on during the week." She followed him out of the cabin and onto the porch.

"How would you know that?" he taunted as he locked up behind them. It was impossible to resist goading her. If he had to react whenever she was around, he liked to prove that she had the same problem.

She stuck her tongue out at him. "My grandma used to watch them."

"Sure, she did." He draped an arm around her shoulders, drawing her down the path that led to the dock. The wood planks echoed with their footsteps as they approached the boat. It was a classic wooden sport cruiser his dad had fixed up when Jesse was still in elementary school.

Lola ran a hand over the polished nose of the boat. "This is gorgeous."

"Thanks. Another of Dad's babies." Jesse picked her up and swung her onto the deck, holding her just a little too long with her breasts pressed to his chest. A tiny smile curved one corner of her mouth, and she brushed her lips across his. He liked that. Even such a simple contact was nice, without automatically leading to sex. Another reaction he wasn't sure was a good thing.

Releasing her, he untied the boat and hopped in. A few minutes later, they were skimming along the lake. Lola grinned, her neck craning as she tried to take everything in. "You must love it out here. It's amazing!"

He'd been here so many times, he almost took it for granted now, but he glanced around and tried to see it from her perspective. It was a beautiful day and there were quite a few people soaking up the sun and enjoying the water. Trees lined the shore and the Sierra Nevadas rose in the distance. It really was amazing—one of his favorite places in the world. He loved it as much for the memories as for the scenery, but he didn't say that out loud.

"We're almost there." He took one hand off the wheel to point toward the long pier that jutted out into the lake. A mishmash of different watercrafts were tethered to the old wood pilings, and he motored them closer until he found an open slip. He shut down the engine and helped Lola out, lashing the boat to a metal tie-off.

She slid her hand into his as if it were the most natural thing in the world, and it felt like it was, which should have freaked him out, but didn't. He shoved the thought aside and walked with her toward the bar. She glanced up at him, eyebrows arched, when they got to the door. "The Spittoon Saloon?"

He shrugged. "Hey, it was named by local miners during the silver rush. They've added TVs and other modern amenities, but it's mostly the same as it was back then."

"Those amenities include real bathrooms, right?" Her eyes widened in exaggerated horror.

Laughing, he held the door open for her. Damn, but he liked this woman. "Yes, princess. There's indoor plumbing."

She wasn't quite sure she believed him as they stepped inside. She'd been to her share of seedy dive bars, but the word *spittoon* in the name wasn't reassuring. A relieved breath eased out of her when she saw it just looked like an ancient cabin with a bar at one end, a few tables scattered around the interior, and a few out-of-place looking big screen televisions. The old mirror over the bar was probably original, and her reflection was wavy as she approached the bartender.

She dug out her wallet, slapped a fifty on the bar, flashing her most charming smile. "I'd like a beer and a channel change, please."

The geezer looked like he was an original fixture too. He grunted. "What kind of beer and what channel?"

"A pitcher of Guinness for me and my friend, here," she replied. Then she nodded toward one of the smaller TVs mounted above the bar. "And if you could just move that NASCAR race over to the big screen, I'd appreciate it."

His eyebrows arched, but he didn't say anything. He grabbed a remote and flipped the channel, then set her and Jesse up with pint glasses and a pitcher of Guinness.

"Thanks, hon. Keep the change." She winked at the old guy, who gave her a gap-toothed grin as he scooped up the cash.

"Any time, pretty lady."

Jesse grabbed the pitcher while she took the glasses, and they headed toward a table near the big screen. He held out a chair for her, amusement flashing in his green gaze. "Does every man alive flirt with you?"

"Yep. And I usually flirt back." She set down the glasses, dropped her purse on the table, and settled in her seat, crossing her legs. The bar was full, but not packed, and she was fairly sure every man there was now staring at the length of her legs that weren't covered by her short skirt. Including Jesse. Ah, well. Let them look. They would anyway, and she'd long since learned to make the best of it. "Do you have a problem with that, Kasen?"

"Nope." He poured them both a pint and then sank into the chair next to hers, draping an arm across the back of her seat. "As long as you're coming home with me, I don't really care."

There was nothing in his expression to indicate he was lying. Another pleasant surprise. Most men she knew took issue with her flirtation, assuming it automatically meant she wanted to have sex with whomever she flirted with. "I don't sleep around, you know. This weekend is a fluke."

He took a swig of his beer, licking the foam from his lips before he met her gaze. "I occasionally sleep around, though I've never brought a woman to the cabin before. So it's a fluke time for everyone."

But he hadn't said he believed her about her sexual history. That stung more than it should, and she focused on the NASCAR race on the TV. She'd missed the beginning, but at least she'd be able to see who won. She kept her eyes peeled for the black car emblazoned with the red Hanley's toothpaste logo. When it swept across the screen, getting bumped hard by the car following it, she jolted in her seat.

"So, are you going to explain why we just *had* to watch a race? Do you have money riding on it or something?" Jesse's tone indicated his disbelief, though whether it was because she might be a gambler or because she'd dragged him out of bed, she couldn't tell.

"Money is the least of my worries on race days." She downed some of her beer. "I'm just hoping my baby sister doesn't get smeared into a wall."

"Sister?" It took him a moment to process that. "Wait, Lola *Adams*. Blake Adams is your sister? Buddy Adams is your uncle?"

"Imagine that." She grinned into her drink. Her sister was one of the few women who'd ever been a NASCAR driver, and she was pretty, which the media loved. That she was related to a racing legend like Uncle Buddy was just the cherry on top.

Jesse frowned. "Why weren't Dean and I told about your history when the network put you on the show?"

She snorted. "I don't trade on my family name, that's why. I look like my mother, so you can't tell from looking that I'm Buddy's niece, and I went into producing to make a name for *myself*. Only a select few of the network execs know I'm from the racing Adamses, and yeah, that probably played a part in them supporting me with *Revved Up*, but there were a lot more people than just the ones who knew that made the final decision. I got the show because I'm good at what I do."

"I..." Jesse trailed off, staring at her as if he'd never seen her before. Maybe he hadn't. All he saw when he looked at her was someone to screw. It shouldn't disappoint her that he was the same as every other man alive, but it did. Just sex. That was all this was. Chemistry and hormones. Just because he was a nice guy didn't mean he'd fallen out of her own-or-bone categories.

"Close your mouth, Kasen." She focused on the screen and watched her sister jockey her way up to tenth place. It was too soon to get excited, but that would be a damn good finish for a new driver. The silence got a little too long, with Jesse still looking at her strangely, so she started talking. "Blake had a crappy run in Talladega last week, so I'm hoping this is a better race."

He cleared his throat. "She's been doing pretty well this year, hasn't she?"

"Damn well, especially for a rookie." She couldn't keep the pride out of her voice. She worried about her sister because there were always dangers out on the track, but Blake was good at what she did. "Uncle Buddy is thrilled, not that he'd ever tell her. He leaves the supportiveness to me."

Jesse shifted in his seat and his arm slid against her back. Awareness skittered over her skin, and that was before his fingers stroked down her shoulder. "What about your parents?"

Hesitating for a moment, she gave him the shortest answer possible. Just sex. No need to get personal. She ignored that she'd had no problem diving into his personal life last night. "They passed when I was fifteen and Blake was twelve. We lived with Buddy after that."

His arm tightened around her, as if he wanted to comfort her. The idea was so foreign, she didn't even know how to respond. Men wanted things from her, they didn't want to *give* her anything. And she didn't lean on anyone, ever. She stood on her own two feet, physically and emotionally. It was safer that way. She'd learned not to depend on people sticking around a long time ago. She felt his gaze searching her face. "So, you were a track brat."

"I graduated and went to college three years later, so not me. Blake, though, yeah. She took to it like she'd been born to be on the track."

"You guys are close?" His fingers drew circles on her shoulder, and tingles flowed in the wake of his touch.

She wanted to hate how quickly his touch could get to her, but she couldn't quite make herself. "Yeah, we are. I took care of her until I left for university."

"Where does she live?"

Taking a deep swig of booze, she attempted to distract herself from the way her body warmed when he put his hands on her. "Her racing team is based at the Atlanta Motor Speedway, which is where Buddy taught us everything we know about cars, trucks, and anything on wheels."

He was silent for a long time, and they both watched the many laps of the race count down. His fingers still slid over her skin absently and she had to squeeze her thighs together to quench the ache that built between them. He didn't even seem to realize what he was doing to her, which made it all the more frustrating.

"So, you really do know your stuff when it comes to cars."

The comment caught her off-guard. His thoughts definitely hadn't followed the same sensual lines that hers had, which annoyed her a little more than it should.

"Don't worry," she drawled, exaggerating her Southern accent. "You're not the first guy to assume I'm all boobs and no brains."

He choked on a sip of his beer, snorting it up his nose. "Jesus, Lola."

"Tell me I'm wrong." She folded her arms, giving him a look that dared him to contradict her. "Tell me you didn't think for even a second that I slept my way into this producer gig."

Setting down his glass, he wiped his face with a napkin. "Okay, yeah. Maybe I did think something like that. But tell me you *don't* use your boobs as much as your brains to make men do what you want. Tell me you're not accustomed to your looks getting you anything you ask for."

"I didn't ask to be born pretty, or to grow big breasts when I hit puberty." At first, she'd been horrified by how much attention her body got from guys. But she'd had to deal with it as best she could. She jutted her chin pugnaciously. "If I have to put up with men drooling all over me, I should get something out of it."

He chuckled. "More power to you."

She narrowed her gaze at him. What was the catch? She'd had variations of this conversation with men she'd worked with *and* men she'd dated, and none of them had ever laughed about the philosophical approach she'd adopted. Her looks were what they were, and they had pros and cons like everything else in life. "You're not going to call me shallow? Say I'm wrong and should wear a burlap sack so men aren't tempted by me?"

"It'd be a shame to cover you in burlap. Probably scratchy for you too." He pulled the basket of peanuts in the middle of their table closer to him, plucking one nut out to crack it open and pop it in his mouth. "Why would I tell you to change anything you're doing now? Your methods apparently work for you."

She stared at him, knowing she shouldn't be so dumbfounded by his reaction, or lack thereof, but she'd had to face resentment and hostility from other people for most of her life, just because she was nice to look at. No one outside her family had ever just accepted her. It confused her and made disquiet roil in her belly. "You surprise me."

"Don't worry." He popped another peanut into his mouth, offering her a wink. "You're not the first woman to assume I'm an ignorant, chest-thumping grease monkey."

She couldn't prevent the laugh that burst out. "Touché."

Chapter 6

Jesse grinned as he watched Lola do an uninhibited little dance in the middle of the bar. He wasn't the only one who noticed. Everyone in the place had been pulled into the drama of the race with her, as she'd tensed every time another driver rubbed her sister's bumper, whooped when Blake passed another car.

Lola was a sight to behold. And the thing that killed him was she didn't even seem to notice or care about the effect she had on all the men in the saloon. His mom would have milked the attention for all it was worth. Lola had focused totally on her sister's race.

"She finished ninth!" She pumped her fist in the air, then smiled when she glanced down at him. Grabbing his face, she popped a quick, hard kiss on his mouth. "Holy crap, do you know how awesome that is for a rookie?"

He nodded. Yeah, he knew enough about NASCAR to understand how big this was. Though he was having more fun watching her do a victory dance than anything else.

Her cell phone rang, and she swooped down on it. "Blake! Of course, I watched it! Don't I always? I'm so *proud* of you, baby sister." She paused, and Jesse could hear shouting and excited chatter on the other end of the line. "Okay, go talk to the press and try not to swear on national TV. You'll make Granny roll in her grave." There was laughter in response to that. "Love you, Blake. Drag Uncle Buddy out to celebrate after. Bye!"

"I take it she's happy."

"Over the moon." She tapped the screen to end the call and slipped the phone back into her purse. "As she should be."

The smile that creased her cheeks was the most open expression he'd ever seen on her face outside of the bedroom. It was clear how much she loved her family, and that was something that resonated with him. He'd worked damn hard to build his family's legacy, enjoyed that he could work with his cousin every day because of the Kasen business.

Cars and family. Who knew two of the things that were most important to him would also rank so high for Lola? She could have spent the day in bed, wallowing in her own pleasures, but instead she'd insisted on making sure she'd been there for her sister the only way she could from halfway across the country. It shook the image he'd formed of her in his head. The real Lola had depth and character, layers that fascinated him. He wanted to know more. He just plain wanted more.

He sat back in his chair. "Ready to go back to my place, or did you want to flirt with the bartender a little more?"

A smoky laugh rolled out of her. "I don't think I have a pressing need to flirt with anyone right now. I'm all yours for the rest of the weekend. No more interruptions."

He liked the sound of that way too much. She was *all his* this weekend. He wondered what that might be like all the time, knowing that she was always *his*, no matter how many men fell over themselves trying to please her. It was a dangerous, temping thought.

Far too tempting.

"All right, let me check out those fancy indoor restrooms you promised me, and then we can get back to the cabin." Sultry heat flashed in her gaze. "And get back to what we were doing before the race."

The sinful expression on her face was enough to scramble what was left of his brain. Watching the sway of her hips as she walked toward the short hallway that led to the saloon's one bathroom did nothing to help his restraint. He lasted all of thirty seconds before he was up and following her.

He braced a shoulder against the wall for the few minutes it took Lola to open the door. She jolted when she saw him, her eyes widening in surprise. "Wha—"

Not letting her finish, he crowded her into the bathroom and slammed the door behind them. With a quick flick of his fingers, he locked it. He wrapped an arm around her waist and pulled her flush against him, groaning at the contact. "I want you."

Her breathing hitched, and he could see her pupils dilate. She licked her lips. "Here? Now?"

"Always." And then he feasted on her lips.

G od, she craved the taste of him. The joyful high from her sister's race fizzed through her veins, and the way he'd primed her by stroking her back and shoulders coalesced into an unstoppable need. He shoved his tongue into her mouth and she sucked on him, biting just hard enough to make him jolt.

His hands skimmed over her breasts to squeeze the heavy globes and tweak her nipples. Fire sparked to life within her, a liquid heat that sluiced over her body and centered between her thighs. Wrapping her arms around his neck, she thrust her fingers into his hair, loving the texture of it against her palms. He moved down to her skirt, pulled the denim up until it bunched around her waist. It wasn't comfortable, but she didn't care when he snapped one of the strings that held her panties together and slipped a finger in to tease her sex.

She threw her head back. "*Jesse*. Hurry!"

"Whatever you want, honey," he growled.

The heavy rasp of his zipper sliding down made her heart leap, excitement twisting inside her. Jesus, they were in a *bathroom*. This was insane. But it was par for the course this weekend. His hard, hot erection brushed against her thigh and a single moment of reality returned. "Condom?"

He paused. "Damn it."

"Uh, I think you can get one right over there." Pointing to the condom and tampon dispenser mounted on one of the walls, she tried to keep in a chuckle, but it emerged as a snort anyway.

He didn't bother to hold back, laughter spilling out as he left her to fetch some protection. "Thank God bar owners are prepared for people doing drunk, stupid things."

"Someone has to be responsible." She held out a hand to him. "Now slide on your responsibility and get over here."

That did nothing to stop his laughter, and his hands fumbled for a moment before he was able to sheath himself in the rubber. But then he was there, pulling her up into his arms, and she wrapped her legs around him. Her panties had twisted awkwardly, but they were out of the way enough to do what she had in mind. She gave him a little smile. "Since we are in a bar bathroom, can we...not touch anything?

I don't even want to know what else people have done in here before us."

"Too dirty for you, princess?" His grin was more playful than mocking, and his hands squeezed her butt, easily holding her up.

"There's dirty and there's dirty." She arched a bit, positioning herself to take him inside her. "I only like the kind that guarantees an orgasm."

"Orgasms are good," he agreed.

Standing in the middle of the room, he pressed upward and eased his grip on her so gravity would impale her on his shaft. The feel of him stretching her was amazing, and the slick glide was sheer, erotic pleasure. Digging her nails into his shoulders, she moaned.

"Hold on tight." He leaned back a bit, then lifted her a few inches and let her drop again.

She tensed her legs to help, raising and lowering herself on his erection while his hands held her hips. She had no idea how he managed to keep them upright, but she wasn't going to stop and ask. They moved together seamlessly, groaning each time he pushed into her. The head of his shaft hit her in just the right spot and tingles exploded over her limbs. Her breathing grew sharp and frantic, her heart pounding so loudly in her ears, it drowned out all other sounds.

The muscles in her thighs burned from the strain, but she ignored the pain. The drive toward climax held her too tightly in its grip for her to stop now. Her sex slapped against his pelvis on every downward pass and each impact made sensation bolt through her like a strike of lightning. She was so close, she could feel completion shimmering just beyond her grasp.

The ragged edge to his breathing told her he was just as close as she was, and that spiked her lust even higher. She loved how they could turn each other inside out. It was crazy and powerful and like nothing she'd ever felt before. He filled her to the limit and her inner muscles clenched around his shaft. Stars burst behind her eyes and she knew she wouldn't last much longer.

"I'm going to come, Lola. Come with me." It was a command, a demand, and it sent her right over the edge.

A small scream broke from her throat, and the walls of her sex closed around his erection. Goosebumps shivered over every inch of her skin, and a hot wave of climax crashed over her. He drove toward his own end, and it dragged out her orgasm. Her channel clenched in rhythmic pulses that made her eyes rolled back.

He slammed inside of her one last time, pulling her to the base of his shaft as he ground himself against her sex. They both cried out, and he shuddered. An aftershock of orgasm went through her, euphoria hitting her in a rush. Giddy laughter spilled from her and she buried her face in his shoulder. He smelled of sex and sweat and Jesse.

"You okay?" He smoothed a hand down her hair.

"Mmm-hmm. Never better." It was the simple truth, and it shook something deep inside her. When had she ever felt this good, connected this quickly with a man she actually *liked*, who treated her well and actually listened when she talked? Never.

And she couldn't keep him. She couldn't depend on this staying good. Nothing ever did. For some unfathomable reason, that made her want to cry. She held him tighter and allowed herself to enjoy the feel of him cradling her in his arms. Just for a little while longer, then she'd let him go.

Chapter 7

The next morning, Jesse sat on the back porch, his chair tipped on its hind legs, his feet propped on the railing. He cradled a mug of coffee in his hands as he stared out at the wide expanse of the lake. Dawn broke and shot light over the water, making the waves sparkle. He sat there thinking for a long time, facing a few truths.

She wasn't like his mother. His mother had been shallower than a puddle, relying on her pretty face to get her whatever she wanted and never wanting to work for anything.

Lola might be pretty, and she might use that to her advantage, but that was where the resemblance ended. She didn't *expect* anyone to hand her anything. She worked hard, she knew her craft, and she clearly loved her family. He couldn't imagine her bailing out on anyone she cared about.

And he wanted to be one of those people she cared about. He wanted it badly.

The thought made his hands grow slick with sweat, and he clenched his fingers around the coffee cup. He hadn't had a serious relationship in his entire life, never willing to commit to someone, knowing he could end up as devastated and alone as his old man. It had been a pretty powerful deterrent. Until now. Until Lola.

Which meant he had to do something about it.

Lola found him lounging on the porch, bathed in the rosy golden light of sunrise, his brows drawn together in thought. It made her chest tighten to look at him, he was so gorgeous. All she had on was his T-shirt, and she tugged on the bottom of it before she shrugged and stepped out to join him. They only had a few hours left, and she wasn't going to worry about a random boater on the lake who might see her half-naked.

"Mornin', sugar."

"Hey." He turned his head to look at her, a tender smile curving his lips and making her heart skip a beat. He held out his coffee mug. "Want some? There's a fresh pot on the counter, but I'm willing to share."

Accepting the cup, she curled up in the chair next to his and took a sip, sighing as the liquid caffeine hit her system. He reached over and she gave him back the coffee. He grinned at her, set the mug on the floor between them, caught her hand, and twined their fingers together. They sat together in silence for a long while, holding hands, and the sweetness of it was lovely. She wished there was a way to keep this feeling, to keep reality at bay forever.

Jesse squeezed her fingers. "I was thinking..."

"I knew I smelled something burning." She rolled her head against the chair until she could see him.

"Funny girl." He shifted, looking uncomfortable for a moment. "No, I was thinking this weekend has been really good."

Something in his tone made her stiffen. "Yeah..."

"What if we didn't limit ourselves to just this weekend?" He turned to face her fully. "What if we wanted this to be a longer-term thing?"

Emotion bloomed within her, hot and beautiful. The word *yes* formed on her lips, but she clamped them shut before she did something incredibly stupid. Reality returned with an ugly crash. If she wanted to be taken seriously with the network, she had to work twice as hard as any other producer. The last thing she needed was to demonstrate how unprofessional she was by getting caught screwing around with one of the men on her show.

"And how would that work? Hiding it from our coworkers, sneaking around? My concerns about us haven't changed. Nothing has changed." Liar. Big, fat liar. *Everything* had changed...except their circumstances.

He frowned, letting go of her hand. "Why would we have to sneak around? Would you be ashamed to be dating me? It's one thing to hide that you're just hooking up with someone, but I was thinking of this as more than a quick booty call whenever we could grab it."

"You were?" She made her tone as dubious as possible.

"Yes."

"And then what happens when we break things off? Then it becomes awkward for everyone to work with us." She shook her head, folding her arms protectively over her chest. "It's not a good idea. We had our weekend, and that probably wasn't a good idea either, but it's done. We can't go back and change things now."

The blood had slowly drained out of his face as she spoke, a muscle ticking in his jaw. "I see."

"Don't be upset, Jesse. This is what we agreed to." She despised the pleading note that had entered her voice. Who was she trying to convince the most? Him or herself? Pain knifed through her, and she hated to reject what he was offering. They fit so well on so many levels, and if things were different—

She cut off the thought. No. Things would never be different. Her decision had been made before she ever came to his little mountain Shangri-la—back when she was clearheaded and logical.

"I know." He swallowed, glanced away. "I just... Wow, we really weren't on the same page. I wanted to move into something deeper, and you're wishing you could go back and erase that we ever happened." A short laugh huffed out of him. "I read that wrong, didn't I?"

"That's not...Jesse..." She reached for him, couldn't stop herself, but he recoiled.

"I need to stow the boat before we leave today. I should probably take care of that now." He stood abruptly, vaulted over the porch railing, and walked away without a backward glance.

She clamped a hand over her mouth and told herself she had no right to cry.

He'd been a fool. Anger at himself and at her roiled through him as he strode toward the cabin, made him want to put his fist through the nearest wall. Even then, the rage couldn't mask the ache that spread within him like a bruise. For the first time in his life, he'd wanted more than a couple of days to burn up the sheets with a woman, and she didn't want him for anything else.

But that was the problem. He'd seen the split second of utter longing on her face when he'd first mentioned the idea of a real relationship. She'd covered it quickly, buried it under justifications, but he knew what he'd seen. Deep down, she wanted this as much as he did, but she was too damn scared of it ending badly to even try.

The irony there was a bitter pill to swallow. Before now, hadn't that always been his role? Anything that got too heavy made him bolt. And he knew nothing he said was going to change her mind, just as no words had ever changed his mind before now. She either wanted it enough to try, or she didn't.

She'd already been clear on her decision, but that didn't stop the agony that pounded through him. It shouldn't hurt this bad for something that had lasted so short a time, but if it hadn't been powerful, he would never have wanted to keep it. He shook his head, shoved a hand through his hair.

Mounting the porch steps, he pushed through the back door and drew up short when he found her in the kitchen, still wearing only his shirt. She rinsed out their coffee cup in the sink, hunching her shoulder as if she couldn't bear to look at him. That just pissed him off even more, and he was across the room in two seconds.

He wrapped an arm around her waist, crowding her forward into the kitchen counter. She sucked in a breath and glanced back, her eyes finally meeting his. "What are you doing?"

"What do you *want* me to do?" The question was a gruff demand, and he locked his gaze with hers, daring her to look away.

Her mouth opened and closed, but no words emerged.

Leaning down until his lips grazed her ear, he whispered, "I want to bend you over this sink and give it to you hard. I want to hear you scream my name and beg me to let you come."

"Yes," she breathed, a shiver quaking her body. "I want that too."

Not bothering with a verbal response, he slid a palm down her stomach and between her thighs, delving into her sex. Flicking his fingers over her little nub, he loved the way it hardened for him. He could smell her desire, feel the way her core grew slick. The way her hips began to undulate, pushing into his touch, made a fierce smile stretch his lips. He used his free hand to grab the hem of her shirt and jerk it over her head, leaving her naked as he threw it to the ground. She shuddered, her chest heaving as her breathing sped. He thrust two fingers into her channel, and a high scream pierced the silence.

"Bend forward." The command was guttural, his voice a mere growl. "Grab the sides of the sink."

It would be an act of pure possession. He knew it, and so did she. That she didn't even protest told him a lot, probably more than she would have liked. She gripped the edges of the sink and leaned forward, a quiver running through her.

Ripping open his fly, he shoved his jeans down and kicked them out of the way. He slapped her backside, and she gasped but didn't move. Nice. He dropped to his knees behind her, taking in the view of her sex, so slick with juices for him she was dripping.

A breath shuddered out of her. "I...I..."

Lola, speechless. There was a first. He snorted and nipped at the lower curve of her buttock, making her jolt.

Bracketing her hips, he held her in place while he flicked his tongue over her slit. The muscles in her thighs jumped, and she squirmed a little, so he tightened his grip. He closed his mouth around her hardened nub and suckled. Lola's cry echoed in the room, and he smiled against her flesh. He ran his tongue up and down her opening, lapping up her cream.

The taste of her was feminine and musky, coating his lips. And he'd never have a moment like this again. Pain speared through him, but he shoved it away. Time enough for that later. He moved his fingers down and inward, teasing her nub. She shuddered and moaned, and he drove his tongue into her pussy, taking her ruthlessly with his mouth. Her inner muscles contracted against his lips, her moans growing louder and more desperate.

Slipping downward, he bit her nub lightly, and her entire body jolted in reaction.

"Oh, my God!" She screamed then, and he felt orgasm thrumming through her.

Now. He had to take her now. Had to leave an indelible mark on her that she'd never forget.

He reached for his discarded jeans, fumbling for his wallet and the condom inside. His hands were actually shaking when he slid the rubber on. He jerked to his feet, more than ready.

"*Please*, Jesse." Lola's hips rocked backward, her body bent in total submission. "Please, please, please."

He liked hearing her beg, far too much. With one hand, he grasped his shaft, sliding the head up and down her wet slit. He used the other palm to swat the fleshy part of her upper thigh, making her squeal. He shoved his erection deep inside her, hilting himself in one rough push.

"Jesse," she breathed.

The soft pleading in her voice was a heady aphrodisiac for him. He loved this. Every second of it. She quivered, arching her back to give him as much access as he could want. He pressed forward and retreated, moving slowly but sliding deep into her with each thrust. It took everything he had to keep from pounding into her hard and fast the way his body urged him to, but he wanted to hold on to these last precious minutes, wanted to hear her scream his name before he was done with her.

"Don't stop," she gasped. "Make me come."

Holding on to his control with a death grip, he maintained his leisurely pace, withdrawing and sinking back inside her. Molten lava flowed through his veins, and each time he entered her, he burned hotter. The threads of his restraint began to unravel and he picked up speed and force, the slap of his stomach meeting her backside echoing loudly in the kitchen. The sound of their heavy breathing and low groans added to the carnal symphony. The way she arched and writhed each time he penetrated her told him exactly how close she was to climax. He took her harder, wanting to push them both over that edge. Reaching beneath her, he flicked his fingers over her hard, little nub.

"Jesse!" She cried out, and the walls of her channel closed tightly around his thrusting erection. Low, animalistic moans spilled from her and he knew she'd reached orgasm.

Letting go of his control completely, he thrust deep into her, rolling his pelvis against the curve of her backside. Heat roared through him, and he came hard. He emptied into her and the sounds of her pleasure only drove his climax onward. It went on forever and ended far sooner than he'd have liked. The best sex of his life, and it had only gotten better each time. And now it was over, and the realization crashed his high.

Her legs buckled and he caught her against his chest, savoring the feel of her for one final moment. Then he forced himself to let her go. Unlike his father, who had never really let go of his mother, even after she left. But Jesse couldn't do that to himself. As much as he wanted to hold on, if that wasn't what Lola wanted—if *he* wasn't what she wanted—then there really was no point, was there?

It could have been amazing between them. It might have been. And the not knowing was what would haunt him the most.

Chapter 8

After she'd showered and washed away the evidence of sex, Lola felt like she could face Jesse and say their last goodbyes before they went back to the real world.

She didn't want to. God, she didn't. It took everything in her to pack her things and carry them out to her car. Jesse was already outside, doing a final check on the repair she'd done on his ride. Of course. She would have done the same. A giggle escaped her, but it sounded more like a sob.

His big body stiffened when she came near, but he didn't look at her, just continued to inspect his engine. She walked slowly to the back of her car and put her bag in the trunk. Then there was no putting it off anymore. It was time to get the awkward, awful ending over with.

Pain throbbed inside her and she wanted to kick herself. Why had she thought she could have a simple affair with this man and walk away unscathed? Too many hormones interfering with her good judgment.

It was a mistake she'd have to live with until the end of the show season. She didn't know if she could make herself stay on after that, not if this horrible, crushing weight on her chest didn't ease up. She shook her head. That was a problem for another time.

She pulled in a deep breath and forced a smile to her face, one bright enough to make her Southern Belle mama proud. "So."

"So," he grunted. Straightening, he closed the hood of his car and wiped his hands off on a rag. When he finally looked at her, his expression was carefully blank.

She wasn't sure if that was a blessing or not. Would she rather he show her his pain or his anger because she'd insisted they stick to their bargain? Maybe. At least it would have been real rather than this false blankness he had on his handsome face.

Making a production out of fishing her keys from her purse, she let them jangle musically in her hand. "So, I'll see you at the garage tomorrow. I think the Shelby Cobra roadster you're doing next is going to shape into a great project. The before and after will be dramatic."

"Yeah." He sighed. "Yeah, I think so too."

He tossed the dirty rag onto the toolbox at his feet, then stowed it in his trunk. Striding past her, he went up to the cabin and locked the door. Then he walked around the building, checking the windows to make sure everything was secure.

Should she wait until he was done, or was he hoping she'd leave now? She wavered, uncertain, unable to leave yet. She didn't want to walk away without saying goodbye. It seemed rude. The excuse was empty, but she clung to it. Of course, she'd stay and be polite.

Surprise sparked in his brilliant green eyes when he came back around the house. Ah. He *had* expected her to leave. Awkward. She swallowed hard and lifted her chin.

"Everything locked up tight?" She smiled again, but doubted it reached her eyes. She slid her sunglasses on for a little bit of protection. Her chest felt so constricted, she wasn't sure how she was managing to breathe through it.

"Yeah, the cabin is closed." He offered her a tight smile in return and moved as if to turn away from her, but he paused and turned back. He caught her hand, facing her squarely. "Thanks for coming this weekend. I enjoyed it."

"Me, too."

His gaze darkened, pain flashing across his expression. "But you regret it."

She shook her head, unable to put into words all that she was feeling, but unwilling to give him hope that she might change her mind about them. "It was just more complicated than I expected."

"Same." He gave her fingers a final squeeze before letting her go and stepping back. "Well, I guess our visit is officially over."

A harsh pang went through her. Over. It was over. Why did that hurt so much? "Okay. Bye, then."

"I'll see you at work tomorrow." He cleared his throat. "Text me so I know you made it home safely."

"I will."

"Thank you. Goodbye, Lola." He nodded, climbed into his car, and drove away.

She stood there for a long time, watching his taillights disappear. Then she slid into the driver's seat of her Mustang, gripping the wheel so tightly her knuckles ached.

Her cell phone blared and she jolted. It took her a moment to react, to dig out the phone and answer the call. She had to clear her throat twice before she could squeeze words out. She kept her tone as light as she could. "Hey, baby sister."

"What's wrong?" The question was sharp, and Lola sighed. She should have known better than to try to fool her family. They knew her too well.

She swallowed, pressed trembling lips together. "Man trouble."

Her sister hummed sympathetically. "Were you stupid, was he, or a little of both? So I know if you need nice mommy or mean mommy."

"It was all me." That weight in her chest, the huge iceberg, seemed to crack, breaking open her heart. "Oh, Blake, I messed up big this time. I fell in love with him." And then she laid her forehead against the wheel and sobbed.

Jesus, he felt like a zombie in one of those bad horror movies. Dragging through the motions, half-dead. Jesse stood in the break room of Kasen's Kustom Automotive and sucked down his fourth cup of coffee for the day. It wasn't even noon yet. His eyes felt gritty and he'd slept like crap the night before. His bed had felt empty without Lola in it. Funny how quickly he'd gotten used to her soft curves pressed against his side at night.

Pathetic. Just like his dad had been after his mom bailed. But Dad had managed to survive and so would Jesse.

"You all right?" Dean came in the room, shutting the door behind him. Concern shone in his gaze.

Jesse didn't even have the fortitude left to lie. His cousin would have seen through it anyway. "No."

Nodding, Dean poured himself a cup of coffee. His voice was far too casual when he spoke again. "Lola looks worse than you do."

"I hadn't noticed," Jesse replied truthfully. He'd stayed as far away from her as possible, afraid he'd do or say something that would make it obvious what they'd done all weekend. He'd promised her discretion and he'd damn well deliver. A sigh seeped out of him, and he scrubbed a hand down his face. "Look, Dean, this time it's not my fault. I didn't do anything to hurt her."

No, it was Jesse who'd been hurt, and he suddenly had a lot more sympathy for the women he'd walked away from over the years.

His cousin didn't ask for details of what had happened, and Jesse was grateful. Dean set his mug down on the counter. "You going to be all right working with her? We can talk to the network if it's going to be a problem."

Jesse thought about it, he really did. But he couldn't do it. He knew Lola had worked hard to be the producer of *Revved Up*, and she was more than qualified for the position. It would hurt her, when she hadn't done anything other than keep up her end of their deal. It wouldn't be right or fair. While the knee-jerk reaction for him was to shove her out of his life, or hurt her the way he was hurting, he just...couldn't. That was the bottom line—he'd rather slit his own throat than cause her pain.

"No, I can handle it." He met his cousin's eyes, so the other man would know he was serious.

The empathy in Dean's gaze was almost more than he could deal with. Dean had had a rough time of it before he and Andi had finally gotten together. Jesse somehow doubted that kind of happy ending was in his future, and it still floored him that he even wanted such a thing. But Lola had knocked him on his backside from day one.

"I'm here if you need me, brother. You know that." Dean clapped him on the shoulder and walked out.

Yeah, he did know that his family always had his back. It had gotten him through the rough times when his mother left and his father died. His cousin, aunt, and uncle had been a bedrock of support. Always had been, always would be. He'd tried to make sure the family business flourished in return. He just needed to keep his focus on the garage until this thing with Lola got easier. He hoped it would, and soon.

But he had his doubts.

The door opened again and Lola stepped into the room. She froze when she saw him, her eyes going wide, and vulnerability flashed across her face before she hid it. He made himself really look at her for the first time that day. He'd avoided it long enough. "You look like hell."

She did. Despite her flawless makeup, she couldn't hide that her eyes were red-rimmed and had dark circles under them. She'd been crying and she hadn't slept. The realization made his heart fist in his chest. She looked about as miserable as he felt, and that said a lot, didn't it? It made him hope. Such a dangerous emotion, but he couldn't stop it.

"Thanks, Kasen." She huffed out a laugh and came in to pour herself some coffee. But now it was her turn to avoid his gaze.

"I'm not giving up on you, Lola. On us." The words were out of his mouth before he could stop them, but he didn't regret them. "You're no happier than I am that we stuck to our weekend bargain, and eventually you're going to get over whatever's stopping you from being with me."

"And you know me so well after a couple of days of sexing it up." Her tone had dropped into a subarctic chill, but he ignored that.

"I know you. I know every curve of your body and what makes you scream, but it's not just the sex. Hell, at this point I wish it were. I've seen how you love your sister, how you swing a wrench, how you do a little dance when you're happy." That got a laugh out of her, as he'd known it would. "I don't know everything, not yet. But I'd like to, if you gave me a chance." He reached out and stroked a thumb down her cheek. Her breath hitched and she quivered, her eyes sliding closed.

"I'll wait as long as you need me to. We've both tried fighting this for months, and it didn't work. I'm betting you won't be able to escape wanting more. I couldn't."

"Why won't you let this go?" Her voice shook when she spoke, a small note of pleading threading through the question.

"Because I love you." The words fell into dead silence, and he wasn't sure who he'd shocked more—himself or her. But it didn't feel wrong to say it. It felt...exactly right. "I love you and I can't pretend I don't. I'm not going to push or force you, or turn into one of those jerks who acts like he owns you." No, it had to be her choice. He couldn't live like his father had all those years, holding on to a woman who had one foot out the door, just waiting for her to leave. "We both want this, I know that, but we have to want it enough to make it work. I'm in. You come to me when you're ready. You know where to find me."

Letting that gauntlet fall, he forced himself to put one foot in front of the other and walk to his office. How long it might take her to give in, he didn't know. Days, weeks, months. He just hoped her resistance didn't last. In the meantime, he had to focus on something else, and work was as good as anything. Dean could deal with the show today. Jesse would handle the day-to-day paperwork that came with running a business. Settling into his chair, he threw himself into the distraction.

Chapter 9

He loved her. It was a litany that repeated in her head all day. He *loved* her. Jesse Kasen, the man no woman had ever kept for more than a couple of months. He was a heartbreaker, as she'd been told within a few days of meeting him. She'd bet every penny she had that he'd never said those three little words to any woman outside his family before.

He wouldn't say them lightly. He wouldn't say them unless he meant them. Those words were serious, and he didn't do serious.

But he sure seemed serious now. He wanted a relationship. With her. After a sleepless night and hours spent sobbing on the phone with her sister, she couldn't dismiss it as easily as she had the day before. It was too big a risk. It was too complicated. If it ended, it would be too messy. She was too busy building her career, and there was no guarantee she'd always be in Reno for work. They were excuses, and flimsy ones. She could make it work, if she wanted to, if she was willing to do whatever it took. Just as he'd said.

Giddiness and fear twisted together within her. She clenched her fists to keep her fingers from shaking.

"You okay, Lola?" The cameraman glanced at her out of the corner of his eye. The concern in his tone made her wince a bit. So much for acting normal and behaving like a professional.

She let a breath ease out of her lungs. She'd been way off her game today, but luckily her crew had covered for her. She owed them one. "I'll be okay, but thanks for asking."

How was she going to be okay? She was so tangled up inside, she didn't even know which way was up. What should she do? Play it safe or take a gamble? She'd already fallen for him, and that was bad enough, but if she let herself rely on him...she'd be utterly devastated when she lost him.

Just like she had been when—

Her heart seized, her eyes closing as agony tore through her.

Just like she had been when her parents died.

Was that what was holding her back? She wasn't afraid of working hard for something important to her. She'd done it when she'd helped Uncle Buddy raise Blake. She did it every day with the show. The hours were long, but she welcomed the challenge. But she'd never relied on anything or anyone the way she'd relied on her parents. Since their death ripped a hole in her world, she'd only depended on herself. And that was what terrified her most about Jesse, wasn't it? He wasn't like the other men she'd dated. He was the kind of man who took care of those who mattered to him. She saw it every day in the way he acted with his employees and cousin. He was the kind of man she could depend on, and that meant if she got attached to him, she could someday suffer that utter agony again, that horrifying, life-changing loss.

She swallowed, blinking back a wave of tears. But...he loved her. Fierce joy whipped inside her. He loved her and she loved him. When was something that wonderful ever going to happen to her again? There'd never been another guy who'd respected her, given her room to be herself, and lit her body on fire the way he did. Could she really run from that?

No.

It didn't matter how terrified she was of losing something so vital to her again, because if she denied herself a shot at the kind of love her parents had shared, she wouldn't really be living, would she? She'd just be running scared from the good in order to avoid the bad, and that wasn't the kind of person she wanted to be.

And she wanted Jesse. She wanted to see where this might go. It could be a disaster or it could be everything she'd ever dreamed of.

She'd take the risk.

Her cameraman was speaking to her again, and she made herself refocus on him. "What was that?"

"I think we're ready to wrap for the day." He took his equipment over to a big black case and began loading it. "The guys are closing up shop and heading home."

She blinked and looked around. The slant of sunlight in the garage told her it was almost evening. When had it gotten so late? She spied Dean putting away a few tools. "Do you know where Jesse is? He disappeared this morning."

She didn't mention that she was the reason for his disappearance, but she was guessing Dean knew.

He slanted a quick, incisive glance at her. "He's in the office."

"Thanks." She turned to walk in that direction.

"Lola?" Dean's voice brought her up short.

She looked back over her shoulder, impatient to get to Jesse. "Yes?"

"Be sure what you want before you go in there." His expression hardened, became unforgiving. "I've never seen my cousin like this, and I don't want you jerking him around. He got enough of that from—"

"From his mom? I know. And I know what I want." She shrugged. "Him."

"Then go get him." A small smile touched his lips, lit eyes that were as green as Jesse's.

She grinned back, butterflies taking flight in her belly as she approached the office. He'd said to come to him, that he wanted her. She clung to that knowledge, praying he wouldn't change his mind. Ever.

Sucking in a steadying breath, she raised her fist to knock and found her hand was shaking. She lowered her arm, and instead of knocking, she put her fingers on the knob and turned it. The door swung in, the hinges emitting a small creak.

Jesse sat bent over his desk, rifling through some papers. "Dean, do you have the invoice for—"

He stopped when he glanced up, and she watched his muscles tighten. She held on to the doorknob like a lifeline and managed to squeak out, "Hi."

"Come on in." He set the paperwork down and leaned back in his chair, his casual pose belying the tension that still hummed in the room. "Did you need to go over something for *Revved Up*?"

"No. Nothing for the show." She stepped into the room and shut the door behind her, then walked over to the desk that faced his. Dean's desk. She perched on the edge of it, and subtly wiped her sweaty palms on her slacks. "I came to talk to you about what you said earlier."

If anything, his body grew tauter. "What about it?"

She opened her mouth, but no words came out. How did she tell him what he needed to know, how scared she was that she'd end up broken and adrift again, why she'd run from his offer of more than sex when she'd wanted to agree so badly she could taste it?

"Lola?" he prompted, one eyebrow arching.

"I love you, too." There. A good place to start. The most important place. "I didn't mean to, and I didn't want it, but I do. So much."

His other eyebrow rose to join its twin, a bit of humor sparking in his gaze. "That's good. I think."

A laugh straggled out of her. "Yes, it is."

He leaned forward, but didn't relax. "I hear a 'but' in there."

"But I'm scared. I'm not good with relationships, haven't been since my parents died. If I depend on a man, he might leave or die on me, and then I'll have to pick up the pieces of my life again." She closed her eyes, swallowed. "I'm strong enough to do it. I survived once, but...it's really hard to look that kind of possibility in the face again." Opening her eyes, she saw he'd risen to his feet, his expression softening with the sympathy that she'd rejected when she'd told him about her parents' death. It gave her the courage to continue. "If I give in to this thing between us..."

"You open yourself up to that possibility." He came around his desk and sat on the front of it, so there were only a few feet of open floor separating them. "I understand."

"Do you?" God, she hoped so, because she wasn't sure she understood it entirely herself.

"I've never committed to a real relationship before, never even thought I'd want to. After what Mom put us through? Christ, no." He ran a hand through his hair, leaving it in furrows. "You think I'm not terrified too?"

That brought her off Dean's desk, and she took a few steps toward Jesse's side of the room. "You are?"

"Yeah." His gaze was more earnest than she'd ever seen it. "But this is too good to walk away from. I know not every woman is like my mother. My aunt isn't. Andi's not. I've just never let myself get tangled up with one of the good ones before." He snorted, his tone turning ironic. "Too wary of falling for the first one I messed with."

Which was exactly what had happened.

"I know exactly what you mean." If she were totally honest with herself, she'd admit that was probably how she'd ended up dating so many jerks. There was no way she'd commit to any of them for long, so her heart was safe. No risk. She'd thought Jesse was more of the same, just the way he'd thought she wasn't the kind of woman he'd fall for. They'd both been wrong. "I don't know what's going to come of this. I don't know if we'll be together for forty years or four months. I just know I love you and I want to be with you right now."

"That's what I want too." He held out his hand to her, waiting for her to take it, waiting for her to be ready, just as he had that first day at the cabin. It was just what she needed. God, she loved him.

Setting her hand in his, she let him draw her forward into his arms. The cessation of pain was so sharp it brought tears to her eyes. It felt good—*right*—to be here with him. Everything settled into place. "I want to make this work, Jesse. I don't want to leave you."

"Thank God." He buried his face in the crook of her neck and she stroked her fingers through his hair. They stood that way for long moments, giving her the chance to savor the way her body fit against his. He felt so good. "I love you, Lola."

It was the most natural thing in the world when their lips met, the soft sweetness soon burning into a sharper need. It was always like this with them. She hoped it always would be. Their tongues twined, the kiss deepening. Tingles rippled down her skin, and his hands cupped her hips, pulling her tight to his body. Some of her muscles loosened and others went taut, readying her for sex. His erection prodded her belly, making her channel contract. The ragged sound of their breathing echoed in her ears. She craved him so much, she pressed herself closer to him and moaned against his lips. They'd drowned themselves in sensuality over the weekend, so going an entire day without touching him, tasting him, had been intolerable. She was addicted.

His hand coasted up her side, curving inward to cup her breast. Her nipples tightened with anticipation, rasping against her lace bra. Excitement sped her heartbeat, heat shimmering through her. He closed his hand over her breast, his fingers zeroing in on the beaded crest, pinching and twisting. Her breath caught and she arched into the contact, craving more, craving that connection she'd only ever found with him.

"More," she gasped.

A low groan was his only answer as he began tugging at her clothes. She did the same with his, pulling his shirt from his pants to unbutton it. Skimming her hands up the plains of his chest was a tactile pleasure. The crisp hair there tickled her palms, and she flicked her nails over his flat nipples. His swiftly indrawn breath made her smile, as did the way he attacked the button on her trousers. She tugged her top over her head and let it drop to the floor. A squeak erupted from her throat when he latched onto her breast, sucking her through her bra. The hot wetness of his mouth, the nip of his teeth, had her up on tiptoes, her fingers digging into his arms to hold herself steady.

"Jesse, Jesse, Jesse," she chanted.

He turned them to pin her against his desk, his leg wedging between hers. She arched into him, riding her sex on the hardness of his thigh. His palms curved over her backside, squeezing, pulling her into fuller contact with his leg. Her nub burned with sensation as she ground herself down and he flexed the muscles in his thigh. It was too much. She couldn't take it. Flames licked at her core, and she wanted him inside her with a desperation that rocked her to her foundation.

Shoving his shirt off his broad shoulders, she tilted her hips to help him push her pants down. Her panties went with the slacks, she stepped out of her heels, and then she was bare except for her bra. Yes. Her hands went to his fly, but he beat her there, wrenching open his jeans and shoving them halfway down his thighs.

"Good enough," he rasped.

He cleared off the desk with a rough sweep of his arm, and then lifted her on to the battered surface. She gasped as the cold metal met her overheated flesh, the contrast intensifying both feelings. She had no idea where he got a condom from—she was just glad he had one. It took only a moment for him to slide the rubber on, then he stepped between her thighs.

She rocked her hips upward. "Inside me. Inside me, please."

"Hell, yes." He hooked her knees over his arms, holding her legs high and wide. The blunt probing of his erection made her whimper with need. He filled her slowly, easing into her tight sheath. Her sex throbbed around his length, the muscles clenching as if to draw him deeper. A shudder wracked his body. He groaned, the sound harsh and loud in the room. Then he stopped.

Embedded deep within her, stretching her exquisitely, he remained still and let the anticipation and tension build. His gaze gleamed as he watched her, knowing it was driving her crazy. She wanted him to *move.*

"Jesse!" She writhed against the hard plane of his desk. "Don't make me wait. I need you."

White teeth flashed in a wicked smile and he nudged his pelvis into her, the rough hair between his thighs stimulating her most sensitive flesh. She mewled in delight, her center fisting once in response. He choked on a breath and finally, *finally* gave in. Bracing his palms on the desk, he leaned over her and forced her legs wider. He withdrew in the same unhurried motion as he'd entered her, then he thrust into her. Hard. Their skin slapped together and she moaned.

It didn't take long for him to pick up speed, and each penetration pushed her toward the blissful oblivion she craved. Her hands scrabbled against the desk, looking for something to hold onto. She gripped the sides of the metal surface, using it for leverage to press herself into his thrusts. Letting her eyes drift closed, she focused on the pure sensation that rocketed through her body.

"Look at me, Lola."

She obeyed and her gaze was snared by the intensity in his. He hid nothing from her, and she could see the same hope, love, and need burning in his gaze that she felt. Her breath caught, emotion exploding through her, twisting with her lust to become something more powerful than she'd ever experienced before. And she let him see it on her face, hid nothing, gave him what he'd given her. It was perfect.

His chest heaved as he sucked in air, and sweat slipped down their skin in rivulets. Climax beckoned, making her limbs quiver. Still, they didn't look away from each other, riding out the firestorm together. He filled her again and again, the angle just right to make her scream. He reached between them, flicking his finger over her nub in time with his thrusts, and she catapulted into orgasm. Her inner muscles contracted around his shaft, milking the length of him. Her back bowed on the desk, a broken cry spilling from her lips.

Lust flushed his face, tightening the skin over his sharp cheekbones. His rhythm grew less smooth as he rode her against the desktop, powering into her. A few more thrusts and he froze, shuddering as he came. "Lola!"

A protracted moment stretched between them while they watched each other come. The lash of need, the rush of orgasm—she could see it all on his face, knew he saw the same on hers. They were in this together, just the way they should be.

He let her legs loose and she propped her feet on the edge of the desk. Leaning heavily on his elbows, he rested his forehead between her breasts, panting for breath. She cupped her hands around the back of his skull, her fingers in his sweat-dampened hair. After long minutes had passed, he lifted his head to look at her, a quiet smile on his face. "I love you."

"I love you too." She grinned, even as happy tears filled her eyes. "We'll make this work, I promise."

The sound he made was rough, and he pulled her close. "I promise, too."

What more could she ask for? Not one single thing. She might not know what the future held for them, but she was smart enough to hang on tight and enjoy the ride. With any luck, they'd keep this thing running for a long, long time.

Forever, if she had her way.

THE END

Want more from C. Jordan? Join her mailing list:

https://www.cjordanbooks.com/newsletter

About C. Jordan

C. Jordan is a California native with an insatiable love for travel. When she's not writing sexy contemporary romance, she can usually be found working as a librarian or wandering the world with her husband.

Also by C. Jordan

Destination: Desire series

A Little Sinful

Never Let Go

Maybe This Time

Wild For You

Forrester Brothers series

A Girl's Best Friend

The Girl Next Door

Unbelievable series

If You Believe

Believe in Me

Make Me Believe

Unbelievable anthology

Revved Up series

All Revved Up

All Tangled Up

Revved Up duology

Excerpt from If You Believe

Cedarville, Oregon

"The end is near!" the grubby man shouted at Aubrey as she walked past. He waved a big sign that said the same thing in fire engine red letters.

The end of what though? The world? America? Poverty? The bad song blasting out of his boom box? She was hoping for that last one as she dumped some change into the rusted coffee can next to him.

"Hi, Jericho." She gave him a wide berth. The homeless guy was certifiably nuts, but harmless, and she'd been forking whatever change she had in her pockets into his can for a couple of months. Every day since he'd parked his unwashed self on the park bench across from her coffee shop Bean There, Done That.

"Howdy, Aubrey!" Jericho gave her a gap-tooth grin before he sobered abruptly, his eyes taking on a weird intensity. "Beware of fire today."

She blinked at him, chills crawling over her skin at the weird statement. Opening her mouth to ask what the hell he was babbling about, she stopped. He'd already started humming along with the radio. Yep, the man was definitely *not* playing with a full deck.

"Yeah, okay. Thanks, Jericho." She waved as she jogged across the street through the early morning fog.

A wave of deep satisfaction rolled through her when she approached the front of her shop. It'd been open for over three years and business was booming. She'd moved to Cedarville from Portland after her divorce was final because she'd needed a change of pace, a change of *place*. She'd caught her ex screwing one of the waitresses at the restaurant they'd owned, so she screwed him in the divorce settlement. Was she bitter? Oh, yeah. Almost eight years as Mrs. Scott Roberts had gotten her nothing except a broken heart and broken dreams.

Scott had cured her of any girlish longings for love and commitment. Now she kept it light and fun with the men she dated. She'd found it was easier for everyone that way. No one got hurt, especially not her.

Unlocking the side entrance, she turned off the security system and went through the routine of opening up the shop. After the chaos and rush of being the head pastry chef at a trendy restaurant in Portland, Bean There, Done That was nirvana. The mornings were her alone time, when the whole world came down to this Zen place with just her, the ovens, and the smell of baking pastries and fresh brewed coffee.

Susan would be in soon to help Aubrey with the morning rush, but this time was all Aubrey's. The time flew by and before she knew it, Susan's massive combat boots were tromping into the kitchen. Glancing up, Aubrey stifled a snort. Over the boots, Susan wore a lacy black Victorian style dress. "Heya, Aubrey."

The only dress code for employees was that they wear a black outfit with the black and green Bean There, Done That apron over it. Susan liked to take the uniform to the next level. "Morning."

The younger woman checked the daily menu Aubrey had written on the chalkboard out front and then took the chairs off the tables to set up for the day. Thirty minutes until they opened. They worked in companionable silence. One of the reasons she had Susan on the morning shift was that she didn't chatter.

Wiping a last bit of flour off her hands, Aubrey turned to Susan before walking into the back room. "I'll grab the last batch of lemon cakes out of the oven if you watch the glaze on the stove."

"Sure thing, boss lady." Susan's braids bobbed when she nodded.

Just as Aubrey flipped off the ovens and pulled out the hot pans, a shriek came from the front. Her heart seized in terror before it leaped into a gallop. Slapping the pans onto the cooling racks, she raced for the other room. Flames danced across the stovetop, and Susan lay in a crumpled heap on the floor. "Susan!"

A customer wandered in the door, and Aubrey rounded on him like a madwoman. "Do you have a cell phone?"

He nodded, staring blankly from her to the fire. "Then go outside *and call 911.*"

Reality seemed to hit him. He jerked his cell out of his pocket, spun, and bolted for the door. She turned back to Susan.

"Oh. God." *OhGodOhGodOhGod.* Sweat ran in rivulets down Aubrey's face, her heart pounding so hard she thought it might explode.

The fire hit a dishtowel that had flopped onto the floor near Susan. No time to grab the fire extinguisher. Dropping to her hands and knees, Aubrey crawled as fast as she could to Susan's side, wrapped an arm around her, and slid her as far away from the flames as possible. The heat rolled over Aubrey, drying her eyes out while every instinct inside her screamed to *run.* To escape the danger. But she couldn't leave the younger woman.

Aubrey hacked and wheezed as the smoke got thicker. Jesus, she needed to get the fire extinguisher. Staggering to her feet, she snatched the bright red canister off the wall. The smoke seemed to follow her, and when she spun she realized that the ends of her hair were on fire. Terror exploded through her and she frantically slapped the flames out, her shriek dissolving into a whistling cough as the smoke burned her throat. A sob bubbled up, but she ripped the pin out of the extinguisher and hosed the stove down with white foam. It went everywhere, all over the stove, her, the counters, her, the floor, her. Smoke boiled up while the flames slowly died out.

Whooping sounded in the air as the whole fire department, an ambulance, and a police car rolled up to the front of the shop. Thank God. Tears streamed from her eyes, as much from relief and residual fear as from the acrid smoke. Her lungs burned like she'd sucked the flames down her throat. She sank to her knees beside Susan and closed her eyes. No way was she leaving Susan alone in here, even if the fire was out.

The firefighters bundled both women up and got them out, slapping an oxygen mask on Aubrey in the process. Smoke inhalation, they said. Yeah, she could believe it. She grabbed one fireman's sleeve. Fire damage and the mask made her sound like Darth Vader. "Will she be okay?"

Mason Delacroix. She knew this man. He ordered a black coffee every day at noon. He nodded down at her. "Yeah. She seems to be doing all right. Looks like she's waking up. We'll know more when they get her to Cedarville General."

Aubrey clamored into the ambulance beside Susan, ignoring the protest from one of the paramedics. What was he going to do, toss her out? They both knew she was going to have to get checked out by a doctor anyway. This way it was one trip for Susan *and* Aubrey.

Only then did it occur to her that her business was trashed. A million details bounced through her head, but she couldn't focus on one of them. Police reports, insurance claims, cleaning up the mess.

God, what a mess. It was too much for her right now. Her thoughts slid away, so she closed her eyes and let herself rest. Just for a moment. Weariness dragged at her very bones, and she hung on to Susan's hand as the ambulance sped through the normally quiet streets of her little town.